To all of the girls and women who have found the inner strength to learn from their experiences and to change their lives for the better.

– Patricia G. Penny

Not Just Proms & Parties

Karin's Dilemma

written by
Patricia G. Penny

Lobster Press™

Chapter 1

"*H*e did *what*?" Karin Vincente stopped in the middle of twisting her hair into a loose knot and stared at her friend skeptically.

"I'm not kidding! Sulley and I were just sitting there watching TV and my dad walked in, sat down across from us, and asked Sulley, 'Have you and my daughter been having sex?' I wanted to die right there on the spot!" Sage scrunched up her empty potato chip bag and tossed it onto the table next to her math book. She slumped against the wooden back of the cafeteria chair and looked up.

Karin shook her head and laughed at her friend's predicament. "I knew there was a reason I was better off without a father. What did Sulley do?"

"What was he supposed to do? He sat there with his mouth hanging open for a second and

7

then he just kind of laughed, hoping it was a joke. Except it wasn't. I told Dad that he should leave poor Sulley alone. If he wants to know about my business, then he should trust me enough to come talk to me, and not humiliate my boyfriend."

"Yeah, like you'd ever tell him the truth!" Karin teased.

Sage rolled her eyes. "He'd probably lock me in the house until I was a shriveled old lady. As it is, he grounded me from seeing Sulley for a week because I was 'disrespectful.' Like embarrassing me wasn't."

Karin groaned and wondered how Sage would ever survive the constant disagreements she had with her father. She seemed to be a perpetual source of worry to him. The more he tried to turn her into the girl he expected her to be, the more she rebelled and became the opposite.

"So here it is Friday, and your weekend is ruined. What are you going to do?"

Sage leaned forward excitedly. "I've already asked my mom if I can go to Isabelle's for the weekend. Sulley is picking me up from her place tomorrow night, and Isabelle will cover for me if they call."

Karin shook her head in wonder. "You must think your parents are stupid. They'll catch you, for sure."

"Whatever. I'll still get to see Sulley," Sage commented. "What are you and Ben doing tomorrow night?"

"Nothing," she admitted. "He's away most of the weekend at an indoor tennis tournament." Karin and her boyfriend, Ben, had been inseparable for the past year, though lately it was difficult to find time to see him. Her need to focus on schoolwork in her senior year of high school and hold down a part-time job was interfering with everything – her time with Ben, her friends, and even sports. "I have to work Saturday night and all day Sunday anyway."

"You've got to get a different job. Convenience store hours are way too inconvenient." Sage caught the absurdity of her remark, and they both laughed together before Karin shook her head.

"I would, but the store is close enough that I can walk to it from our apartment. I don't want to work so far away that I have to take a bus. That would be awful."

"And you're too cheap to pay the fare," Sage reminded her.

"Yeah, that too."

"You should get a loan from Ben," Sage said

matter-of-factly. "His mother is a doctor, so he's got lots of money."

Karin snorted her objection and waved her hand dismissively. "No, his *parents* have the money! Ben doesn't even have a job. With the band, the tennis team, and student council, he's way too busy to work."

"Oh, like you aren't?"

"Not anymore. I quit my teams today – hockey *and* basketball." She toyed with her rings so that she could avoid Sage's expression. "I got a C on my chemistry test. I figured I'm trying to do too much, so I told the coaches I had to quit."

"Mid season? Are you kidding? You loved being on those teams."

Karin sighed. She knew Sage was right. It had been an impulsive decision, one that she hadn't discussed with anyone first, but she had felt as though she had no other option.

"And you were one of the best players on the basketball team. Even though you're smaller than some of the others, you're feisty and quick," Sage continued.

Karin pushed aside her own doubts about what she had done and tried to explain. "I have to be one of the top applicants or I won't get a scholarship. My mother really can't afford to help me pay any tuition, and I have to get a degree or I'll never be able to support us both."

"Look, you're not responsible for your mother."

"But I am. Ever since my dad left her, we've always had to struggle and worry. If I can get a decent education and become a veterinarian, then I'll earn a good salary and be able to make both of our lives easier."

"Whatever happened to your idea of just finding her a nice man?" Sage teased. "Somebody with a decent job so you can stop worrying about her, like ... that new economics teacher!" She pointed eagerly toward the door of the cafeteria where a nice-looking guy in his forties stood talking with a student. "*He* looks like someone who could keep her occupied when you go away to school."

"You make it sound like she needs a babysitter! No, I just wish she could find someone that she'd really enjoy spending time with – someone to take her out for dinner, or to a movie." Karin sighed. "But she just isn't interested in dating. So it *is* up to me to take care of her. It isn't just *my* life that depends on this scholarship; it's hers too. I have to start studying more."

"So much for us having any fun together," Sage complained.

They gathered their books from the table, tossed their garbage into the pail, and left the lunchroom. As they made their way down the hall, Sage stopped at the door of her class and pulled Karin's sleeve.

"Monday," Sage said conspiratorially. "We'll have one last fling before you geek out on me. We're going to skip our classes and go shopping, or to a spa. Anywhere but here."

"Skip the whole day?" Karin asked, turning with a skeptical expression. "I don't know – "

"You *have* to," Sage said with finality. "You'll go insane if you don't have some fun. Do you want to be like *her*?" She pointed at Tamara Watson, a girl in Karin's biology class who always carried a briefcase and wore sensible shoes.

"Okay, okay! I'm in," Karin laughed in agreement. "But I'll call you on Sunday to make sure that you haven't already been grounded for life by then!" She headed to biology class, wondering why she always let Sage talk her into these things.

At the end of the day, Karin was disappointed to see that Ben wasn't waiting by her locker. She dropped her schoolbag to the floor and opened her locker to find a note taped to the shelf. "Sorry I missed you. I forgot our law class was going to the courthouse this afternoon. I'll talk to you Sunday after I get home from the tournament. Hope you have a good weekend. Love you! B."

She folded the note into her pocket dejectedly and glanced at herself in the mirror she had put on her locker door. Her dark eyes looked a bit tired lately. Her thick hair had been styled in the morning, but it was out of control now. She patted it down futilely before turning away to look through the books that were neatly stored on extra shelves she had put in her locker. She selected a couple of texts that she would need for the weekend and placed them carefully in her bag. Then she pulled one more so that she could read ahead.

"Vincente!" She looked up and saw her friend Isabelle, who was the center on the basketball team. "I'll see you at the library later," Isabelle called out. "Oh, and they just changed our practice on Monday to four o'clock." Isabelle turned and headed toward the stairs with some other girls. Karin almost called after her but decided to let her go. If Karin couldn't get up the nerve to tell her tonight that she had quit the team, Isabelle would find out soon enough when there was one less person at practice on Monday.

Following the stream of students heading toward the door, Karin stepped outside and was surprised to find that the sun was shining warmly, even though it was still weeks before spring would arrive. She saw the line of school buses waiting in the driveway and decided to hoof it. She had worn her boots and figured the forty-minute walk home would do her good.

She followed the busy main street through downtown, then turned and walked a few blocks to an older residential area. The buildings she passed had once been stately homes, but now most were converted into apartments – some duplexes, some triplexes. It was a tired neighborhood, almost run-down. She hated the thought that she would be leaving her mother here alone when she went away to school.

More reasons why I need to get that scholarship, she thought ruefully. *If I don't, I'll be lucky to ever find a job paying much more than Mom's, and we'll end up in this neighborhood forever.*

She crossed the road and walked toward the brick building where she and her mother lived on the top floor. Their landlord, Joe, was outside shoveling the snow from the side entrance to his apartment on the first floor.

"Hi, Joe," she called as she approached, trudging through the wet snow on the unplowed sidewalk. He answered cheerfully, probably appreciative of the distraction. She smiled at him as she passed and headed for the driveway at the side of the house.

When she rounded the corner, she was startled to see an unfamiliar car in the wide parking area next to her building. It was a rusty white Sunfire with a dented rear fender, parked precisely in front of the sign for apartment number three, the apartment she and her mother shared.

Who's here? she wondered. The parking spot was seldom occupied; her mother was a private person with few friends and hadn't owned a car since Karin's father had left them eight years before.

"Your mother has a guest – a man," Joe said unexpectedly from behind her, causing her to jump. She turned and saw him leaning on his shovel, his ruddy face grinning with the enjoyment of sharing the news.

"A man?" Karin asked in amazement. "Are you sure?"

Joe winked and waved toward her door. "Go see for yourself," he suggested and knocked the snow from the blade of his shovel before heading back to his work.

Karin pulled the door open and headed up the covered wooden stairs. She was excited, but apprehensive, about meeting the first man her mother had ever invited over.

Chapter 2

"Hi, Mom," Karen called as she stepped into the kitchen.

"We're in the living room," her mother answered with unusual brightness.

Karin dropped her backpack next to the shoe mat and pulled off her coat and scarf, taking note of the worn bomber jacket hanging on the rack and the men's boots placed next to her mother's. Crossing the kitchen floor in her socked feet, she went into the other room, feeling awkward as she stood looking at her mother and the unknown man sitting on the couch.

"Karin, this is Calvin Etherington. Cal. Maybe you remember me mentioning him before. Cal works with me."

"Hi, Cal. Nice to meet you." Karin smiled

politely and leaned across the coffee table to shake his hand, which was extended toward her.

"Yeah, you too." He half rose from his seat to greet her. He was short – shorter than Karin's five feet six, and his frame was so slight that she felt her own 120 pounds could take him in a wrestling match. He was wearing navy pants – old ones, maybe polyester – and a rumpled yellow dress shirt that made his face seem sallow. The clothes hung loosely on him. "I've heard a lot about you from your mother."

He smiled as he worked Karin's hand up and down like a slot machine handle. His gray eyes were probing as they rose to hers; she looked away uncomfortably and pulled her hand free.

"All good, I hope," she answered, a little embarrassed to know that her mother had been talking about her at work.

"Absolutely!" He sat back on the edge of the couch and leaned forward, hands clasped, elbows resting on his spread knees. There was an open beer on the table in front of him as well as a plate with the last of some crackers and cheddar cheese. "Your mother can't say enough nice things about you. She's got you up on a pedestal so high that your nose must bleed." He laughed at his joke, and her mother laughed with him and touched his arm lightly. But his laughter died when he saw that Karin didn't appear to be amused. "I hear you're in your last year of high school," he said, reaching forward to pick up his beer.

Karin shrugged. "Last year of high school, but then I'll have seven years of university to become a vet. I'm preparing my applications now."

"I told you that Karin's an excellent student," Brenda said proudly. "We're hoping she may be able to get a scholarship."

"You'd better get one, considering how much tuition they're asking for these days," Calvin snorted as he put a couple of pieces of cheese onto a cracker and popped everything into his mouth. He chewed for a moment and then took a swig of beer. "You sure won't get to university on what our company is paying your mother. It's not much more than minimum wage."

Karin watched as her mother pulled a decorative pillow onto her lap and fidgeted with the tassels. "I don't expect Mom to pay for my education," she said as she looked back at Cal. "I'll either get a scholarship or a student loan. Either way, I'll be responsible for school."

"We've talked about this ever since she was a little girl," her mother confided. "I don't want to see her potential go to waste. I'd hate to see her end up in a job like mine."

Calvin chortled and continued to belittle the telemarketing jobs that he and her mother held.

"There's nothing wrong with your job, Mom," Karin murmured, disturbed that anyone would make her mother's work sound insignificant. Positions were hard to come by, especially since her mother had never completed college. After an earlier lay-off, her mother had been happy to find work eight months ago.

"It pays the bills," her mother conceded. She patted the couch. "Why don't you come and sit with us for a while, honey?"

Karin glanced at Cal, who was smirking confidently as he leaned back into the cushions, one arm outstretched across the crocheted blanket on the back of the couch, fingers extended toward her mother's shoulder. One of his feet was up on the coffee table, his gray wool sock starting to wear thin at the heel.

"I'd like to, but I've got some homework to do and I'm meeting Isabelle at the library later," she said apologetically. "I'll just make a sandwich and have it in my room. It was nice meeting you, Cal."

"Yeah, you too." He rose to shake her hand again, looking genuinely pleased to have met her.

"Maybe I'll see you again sometime."

"Maybe."

She headed into the kitchen and closed the door behind herself, listening to their voices carry. She heard him say what a nice girl she seemed to be and what a good job her mother did raising her alone. Her mother sounded embarrassed as she thanked him. She didn't take compliments well, never having heard very many during her marriage. Karin could picture how her mother looked right now – undoubtedly flushed, with her eyes lowered.

Karin pulled a can of tuna from the cupboard and started to make herself a sandwich, wondering why her mother had invited Calvin over. Her mother had not dated at all since Karin's father had left them. Although her mother was not unattractive, her posture reflected a desire to be unnoticed and her old-fashioned, modest style of dress made her seem mousy and older than her thirty-eight years. She had never suggested to Karin that she had any interest in finding a boyfriend.

She heard her mother's laughter from the living room. It was uncommonly girl-like, flirtatious. The rare sound made Karin realize how long it had been since she had heard her mother truly happy. She sounded like a different person.

After a few minutes, the kitchen door swung open and her mother walked in smiling. "Cal needs another beer," she said, as much to herself as to Karin as she opened the fridge and took one from the shelf. She gave Karin a quick squeeze of excitement and then went back into the living room, leaving the door ajar. Karin could see Calvin leaning back into the couch, legs bent, knees apart, looking settled and content, as though the apartment was his own. Her mother handed him the beer and as he reached for it, Karin saw his eyes look toward the kitchen to meet her own. She smiled guiltily, embarrassed at having been caught watching from the other room, and pushed the door closed between them.

She finished making her sandwich and went to her bedroom. She didn't usually like to eat in there; her room was what Sage liked to describe as "neurotically clean." Karin preferred to think of it as "organized," with separate containers for her sharpened pencils and her multi-colored sticky notes. A large bulletin board held her sports ribbons and medals. Her trophies were lined on a shelf in chronological order. "The neatest room in the house," her mother always said. Karin put a napkin onto her night table before resting her glass of juice down.

"Hi, Pippy," she said, leaning toward the cage that sat on a small table in the corner of her room. The tan and white hamster looked up at her with anticipation, and Karin tore a small piece of lettuce from her sandwich and held it through the metal grating for him. He nibbled at it quickly, pulling it eagerly from her fingers.

She had felt a little uncomfortable intruding on her mother and her new friend, so giving them some space seemed like the right thing to do. But after all these years of wishing that her mother would find a nice man to date, she had to admit she was disappointed that *this* was the man. Still, Sage *had* suggested that a boyfriend would take the worry away from leaving her mother on her own in the fall. Maybe this was all for the best.

As she settled on her bed and took a bite of her sandwich, Cal's snorting laughter carried throughout the apartment. She rolled her eyes and wondered what her mother could see in that man.

* * *

Almost two hours passed before Karin heard Calvin go downstairs and close the lower door. When she was sure he was gone, she came out of her room and went to the kitchen to slip into her boots for the walk to the library.

Her mother came in carrying empty beer bottles. Her face was flushed slightly and she was smiling with obvious pleasure. "Well, what do you think? Did you like Cal?"

Karin couldn't help but notice her mother's eager face as she awaited an answer. She looked younger than she had the day before, as though her worries had been forgotten for once. Karin was reminded of how she herself had felt when she first starting going out with Ben, how her chest had felt warm and full at the mention of his name, how her heart had pounded when she caught sight of him coming toward her. Her mother deserved a chance to find that kind of happiness. Maybe Calvin could be the one to help her find it. Her own impression of him was only based on a brief introduction. Maybe it wasn't fair to judge him too harshly.

"Uh-huh," she nodded, her chest feeling heavy with the weight of the lie. "He seems okay."

Her mother seemed satisfied with the answer as she crossed the room and hugged her. "I'm glad. I really hoped you would like him. So you're off to the library now?" she asked, taking a scarf from the coat tree and wrapping it loosely around Karin's neck.

"Yeah. And we might get a coffee after." Karin zipped her coat and picked up her gloves. "I won't be late."

"It's too bad Cal had to leave," her mother sighed. "Maybe I should call him later."

Karin frowned. "You don't feel like being alone? I could call Isabelle and meet her tomorrow, if you want me to ..."

"No, no. I was only kidding. You go and have a good time. You know I've always been fine on my own. I'll just work on my crocheting."

Karin was relieved that Calvin would not be coming back to spend the evening alone with her mother. She said goodbye and started quickly down the long flight of wooden stairs to the outer door. As she stepped outside into the cold night air, a brisk wind cleared her head and lifted the sense of unease that had enveloped her when she first met Cal. She pulled her hat down over her ears and started toward the bus stop. She had probably been worried about nothing. He had simply dropped over for a drink after work. It meant nothing. Her mother may never see him outside of the office again. Or so she hoped.

Chapter 3

It was soon apparent that Cal was *always* going to be around. He arrived on Saturday morning to take her mother grocery shopping. After helping her carry in the groceries, he had stayed for lunch, and then he and her mother had settled onto the couch and watched three *Rocky* movies in a row, making it impossible for Karin to exist in the apartment without having to see him. After spending most of the day in her room, she looked forward to going to work in the evening, leaving the two of them playing cribbage at the kitchen table. It was a relief to come home at midnight and find that he had finally left.

Karin rose early on Sunday morning and worked at the store until four o'clock. When she walked home and found the familiar car in the driveway, she resigned herself to spending the rest of the evening in her room – again. After coming in and chatting politely with her mother and Cal for a few minutes, she checked her watch and excused herself to go use the phone. "Ben should be home from his tennis tournament by now," she explained.

She dialed his number as she settled onto her bed for what would probably be a long evening. "I'm so glad you're home!" she said when he answered. "Did you win?"

"Fourth," he said. "But it was a huge tournament so I was happy with that. We had a great weekend. How about you?"

She lowered her voice and filled him in on her mother's new relationship.

"Isn't that a good thing? It's about time that your mom found someone," Ben said. "Do you like him?"

"Yuck! No! He reminds me of a rat." She scrunched her face and shuddered.

"No George Clooney, huh?"

She laughed at the comparison. "You'd have to see him to know how funny that actually is."

"Well, they can't all be as good-looking as me," he joked. "So this is the first guy your mother has dated? I guess it's normal to be a little bit jealous."

Karin stared at the phone in amazement and her voice rose. "You think I'm *jealous*? You are so wrong!" Realizing that she may be overheard, she took a deep breath and dropped her voice to a hush again. "I *want* my mother to find a boyfriend. I've been trying to get her to date forever. When my father first left, I thought she could never make it on her own. You know what she's like – sort of nervous and unsure of herself. I just thought she needed someone to take care of her. I used to try to fix her up with single men all the time."

"You *pimped* your mom?" Ben asked in mock horror.

"Very funny! She was just so shy. She hardly ever left the house when I was young, and she never even considered working until Dad left. Now she really isn't qualified to do anything that pays well, so it's been hard for her – dumped by my dad, turned down by most of the companies she applied to. She still doesn't have a lot of confidence." She sighed and her mouth twitched in a reluctant smile. "I guess you could be right about me being a tiny bit jealous – it's been just the two of us for a long time. But believe me, I'm all about seeing her married again. Just not to this guy. Not *Cal*vin."

"Well, no one said they're getting married. She's only been seeing him for a few days, right?"

"You're right. I'm probably anticipating the worst." She bit her lip and stared at herself in the mirror over her dresser. "Ben?"

"Yeah?"

"You know we're going to end up at different schools next year, right?"

"I know. I don't want to think about it."

"Me either." She thought about it anyway. "I'm really going to miss you. Who else am I going to turn to when everything starts to suck so badly?"

"Why? What else is wrong?"

She filled him in on the bad mark she'd received in chemistry and let him know that she had quit her hockey and basketball teams. He was surprised and asked if she had thought this through. Her voice trembled as she defended her decision. Ben apologized and told her that she was right, she had to do what felt best for her under the circumstances. But she still felt unsettled. When they finally finished talking, she stared at the phone and sighed. She hadn't been completely honest with him about how worried she was. She wondered if he could really understand. How could anyone understand unless they knew what it was like to have their future depend on the decision of a scholarship selection committee?

She flipped her text book open and tried to study, but it was hopeless. She needed cheering up. She slid off the bed and went over to Pippy's cage, lifted him out gently, and held him up to her cheek. "At least we're getting to see lots of each other lately, right, little guy?" she murmured to him softly. She lay back on the bed, resting Pippy on her chest, then picked up the receiver and called Sage.

"Hey, you." Sage had call display on her cell phone, so there was no surprising her.

"Hi, Monkey," Karin answered teasingly, despite her less than stellar mood. Sage had once danced like a chimp in order to scare off an un-attractive, persistent guy at a school dance. Karin loved calling her "Monkey" ever since.

"What's up?"

"My mother's up!" Karin said immediately, dropping her voice. "You should see her. I'm talk-ing makeup *and* perfume. When have you ever seen my mother in makeup?" She didn't wait for an answer. "She's sitting in the living room right now with a *man*! Don't get all excited about it though. I'm using the word 'man' pretty loosely. He's gross. A total loser." Karin rolled back on her bed and sighed.

"Oh, bummer for your mummer."

"'Bummer for my mummer?'" Karin cracked up. "You're such an idiot."

"I know. That's why you like me. Where'd she find him?"

"At work. That's the only good thing about the guy – he works. You should see him, Sage. He's a scrawny little man with freaky eyes. His teeth are yellow. I think he bites his nails – "

Sage was snorting with laughter at the other end of the line. "*Ooh*, he sounds great! Does he have, like, a son, or a brother or something for you?"

"Sure, go ahead and laugh. He's not trying to get with *your* mother."

Sage was still laughing, but she tried to sound more supportive. "I'm so sorry. But don't worry about him. Your mom isn't going to get serious about somebody like that. If he's as bad as you say, I bet he doesn't last a month. She's not desperate or anything. In fact, I always kind of got the feeling that she didn't even want to be with anyone."

"I guess you could say that." Karin had

never talked about her father, even with Sage, but what happened with her father helped explain why her mother had been so disinterested in dating. "When my dad left Mom for someone else, it didn't do a lot for her self-esteem." She caught herself twisting a tendril of hair around her finger and pulled her hand away, tucking it under her legs against the mattress.

"So maybe this guy will be good for her, then," Sage said reassuringly. "It could help her build up some confidence. He might be really nice, once you get past the bad breath or whatever else you find wrong with him."

"Yeah, maybe," Karin answered doubtfully, reaching to catch Pippy before he could fall off the edge of the bed. "He creeps me out though. He showed up at yesterday morning without calling or anything. I was still in my pajamas, so I ducked into my bedroom when Mom let him in."

"I wear pajamas around the house all the time, no matter who comes over." It was true. Plaid pajama pants had never gone out of style as far as Sage was concerned. She'd been known to wear them pretty much anywhere without caring what anyone thought.

"You wouldn't wear them around Cal. He's too weird. Anyway, he brought caramel sundaes over for us, so Mom must have mentioned to him that caramel is my favorite. He's trying to make an impression on her by sucking up to her daughter. Classic move."

"Well, there you go. At least he doesn't show up empty-handed. Enough about you – do you want to hear *my* good news?" Sage's voice was a clear indication that her news wasn't good at all.

"Uh-oh. The overnight at Isabelle's didn't go so well, right?"

"Oh, how did you guess? She's ticked off about you quitting the team, by the way. I thought you would have told her already, so I mentioned it."

"That's okay. I just figured she'd hear about it Monday with the rest of the team. Thanks for telling me though. I'll call her later. So what happened with your plan to see Sulley?"

"I'll spare you the sordid details, but the night ended with me coming back to her house to find my father waiting for me in the living room with Isabelle's mother."

"Shut up!"

"Seriously! He told me to stop seeing Sulley."

"Like you won't see him at school," Karin reminded her. "Speaking of school, I guess the plan for us to skip tomorrow is off now, right?

You're in enough trouble already." She was relieved. Skipping was a stupid thing to do.

"Are you kidding?" Sage asked, eliminating any hope Karin had of backing out of the plans. "I've been looking forward to this. Besides," she admitted sheepishly, "I already told Sulley he should meet us at the bowling alley tomorrow at one-thirty. That'll give us the morning on our own to shop."

Karin laughed with a mix of admiration and worry for her friend. "You just tempt fate, don't you? What if you get caught skipping? Your dad must be just about ready to give up on you."

"That's what I'm hoping," Sage agreed. "If he gives up, I should be able to do whatever I want, right? My mother has already decided I'm a lost cause. She barely asks what I'm up to anymore because she's afraid she won't like the answer."

"My mom likes to know what I'm doing all the time, and with who," Karin told her. "It's only fair. I mean, I want to know where she is and who she's with too."

"Yeah, well, she's in your living room with scuzz man."

"Thanks for reminding me."

The phone connection cut for a split second. "I've got another call," Sage said apologetically.

"Hold on for a sec."

"No, that's okay," Karin offered. "Go ahead and take it."

"Okay. I'll meet you at the mall at nine. And tell your mom that you've filled me in on the new guy and I said she can do way better."

"Yeah, okay."

Karin shut off the phone and tossed it onto the bed beside her. Her mother's laughter trilled again from the living room. Karin shuddered, reached down to the bottom of the bed for Pippy, and then returned him to his cage. He ran into a corner and dug into the wood shavings with frustration, strewing them across the cage. "I know how you feel," she said sympathetically before she picked up her book and opened it to the page where she had left off. She hoped that she could concentrate knowing that Cal was out there winning her mother over with his oozing charm and incredible looks.

She had a lot of work to do if she was going to miss a day of school. She should never have agreed to skip. Now she was going to have to study until midnight. Her head ached just thinking about it.

Chapter 4

"So you expect me to believe that all of you were sick, all three of you, on the same day? Quite a coincidence, isn't it?" the vice-principal, Mr. Pettipas, suggested on Tuesday morning, his hands pressed together as though he was praying.

"We must have all caught a bug at the same time," Sage said seriously, trying to look concerned. "There must be something contagious going around. I didn't get a flu shot this year – did you, Karin?" She looked at them with such a solemn expression that Karin could hear Sulley catch his breath to keep from laughing. He started to cough, his hand flying up to cover his mouth.

Mr. Pettipas sighed as he leaned on his desk toward Karin. "Ms. Vincente, I've already confirmed with your mother that this note you gave us," he gestured disdainfully toward the slip of paper on his desk, "was not written by her." He caught her eyes and held them for a long moment as if to assure himself that she was listening. "I've talked to her about the situation and we have agreed to let this go with a warning. You are an excellent student, and I understand from Mr. Dabney that you have missed a pop quiz. Perhaps the repercussions of that will be enough to teach you where your priorities must lie."

Karin nodded and murmured her thanks, though she wasn't feeling very grateful about the marks she lost or the fact that she would have to face her mother later.

"Mr. Sullivan, Ms. Lewis, I also spoke with your parents. Interestingly enough, not only are the notes you so kindly presented us with today not written by them, but *none* of these notes," he pulled a number of papers from a file folder on his desk and tossed them forward, "*none* of these is written by your parents. Not one. Imagine that."

Sage reached out and examined each of the notes as if she was seeing them for the first time. "I don't understand," she said, looking puzzled at the possibility that someone could have forged a note from her mother. Sulley coughed again.

"Choking, Mr. Sullivan?" Mr. Pettipas looked as though he found the concept mildly pleasing.

The door opened. "Sage's parents are here," the secretary advised. "Should I send them in?"

"Oh, please do," Mr. Pettipas smiled. "You can go now, Karin. I trust I won't need to see you in my office again. Mr. Sullivan, you can wait outside until your parents arrive."

Karin and Sulley rose and stepped around their chairs. Sulley brushed a hand over Sage's shoulder as he passed, and then he and Karin stepped into the main office.

"Hi, Mr. and Mrs. Lewis," Karin said quietly, looking down in embarrassment.

"Karin," Mr. Lewis acknowledged curtly. Sage's mother smiled sadly. They both watched as Sulley made his way across the room and sat down on a chair against the opposite wall.

"Sorry, Mr. Lewis," Sulley said, rubbing his forehead as though he had developed a sudden headache.

The Lewises stood to go into the office where Sage waited. "It's a bit too late for sorry, don't you think?" Mr. Lewis said dismissively. He took his wife's arm and ushered her into the vice-principal's office. The door closed firmly behind them.

* * *

There were two voicemail messages when Karin got home. One was from her mother, telling her that she had received a call from the school and would be home by four-thirty to talk to her about skipping school. The other was from Ben, asking how her day had gone and saying he would call again after band practice and his tennis lesson.

She glanced at her watch. It was four o'clock – half an hour before her mother would be home, half an hour alone to catch up on her schoolwork. She fell back into a corner of the couch and opened her books, grateful for the time alone. Within minutes, she heard the door open and her mother coming up the stairs.

"Hi, Karin! Cal drove me home, so I've asked him in for a coffee." Karin looked up and saw him stepping into the kitchen behind her mother. "It doesn't mean we won't be having a talk later about that call I got from the school," her mother warned.

Karin nodded and closed her book. So much for getting anything done, she thought. "Hi, Cal."

"Hey there! I hear you took a little vacation," he laughed. "You're starting to act like I did when

I was your age." The thought of having anything in common with him made Karin grimace, but he didn't seem to notice. He hung up his coat and then stood in the doorway between the living room and the kitchen, rubbing his hands together and shivering exaggeratedly. "Heater in the car isn't working too well," he explained, turning and putting his hands on her mother's waist, tucking them quickly under her sweater for a second, which made her shriek.

"Cal!" She leapt back from him, laughing, and turned away to make the coffee.

"I'm going to my room to do homework," Karin told them as she rose from the couch, slightly embarrassed by the exchange.

"Again? You're the only kid I've ever seen who does homework all the time," Cal pointed out. She noticed that he had a small scar under his left eye. It was even whiter than the rest of his washed-out complexion.

"Why don't you do it later?" her mother suggested as she came up beside him. "Cal isn't staying long."

"No. I really do need to do this. Sorry." She saw a flicker of disbelief and disappointment from her mother. Picking up her book, she went to her room and closed the door.

Karin was tired of feeling as if she had to shut herself away for privacy. *It's my apartment, not his*, she thought to herself. *It isn't fair that I should be holed up in this tiny room all the time.*

I have to find a way to keep Mom from getting serious about Cal, she decided, but as she listened to the now all too familiar chatting in the kitchen, she wondered if it was already too late.

Chapter 5

"Cal's coming over. He's bringing dinner," Karin's mother told her when she got home from work the next Saturday evening.

Karin flinched. "Again?"

"Is that okay? You don't sound too happy about it."

"Oh, no, it's fine. I'm just surprised. You don't usually have much company so, you know, every day ..." She opened the fridge and surveyed the contents in an effort to keep her mother from seeing her expression.

"Are you upset about me seeing him, sweetheart? I mean, I know it must be hard for you, because it's been just the two of us for so long." Her mother turned her around and kissed her cheek. "I still love you the best," she

41

said teasingly.

"I know. It's okay. It's just that he's here so often." She realized what a whiner she sounded like. "What are you going to do tonight? Is Cal taking you out somewhere?"

"No, we'll be here, watching TV."

"Oh. Ben is coming over to watch a movie." Karin had hoped she and Ben might have some time to themselves.

"Oh good," her mother said. "I was hoping you'd be home so you could get to know Cal better. I've been worried that he might think you're avoiding him. And this way he'll get to meet Ben."

"Yeah. That's great." *Ben will be thrilled*, she thought.

When Ben arrived an hour later, Karin went to the door to let him in and saw Cal coming up the stairs behind him.

"Look who I met in the driveway," Ben grinned, gesturing toward Cal before stopping to give her a quick kiss.

"Who wants pizza?" Cal asked. He passed Karin the boxes so he could unzip his coat.

"Come in, come in," Karin's mother fluttered, waving at Ben and Cal to take a seat in the kitchen. "Did you boys introduce yourselves?"

"Oh, I knew Cal right away from all that Karin has told me about him," Ben assured her. He looked over at Karin with a twisted smile and she had difficulty suppressing a laugh. "Actually, Cal," Ben continued, "you look kind of familiar."

"Oh yeah?" Cal dismissed. "I doubt we've had much of a chance to run into each other."

"You know where I know you from?" Ben smacked his hands on his knee. "The courthouse! I saw you in the lobby there when I was visiting recently with my law class."

"You're kidding!" Karin said aloud, the words falling unchecked from her mouth. If Cal had been to court, there had to be a good reason for it. He was no lawyer, so it probably meant that he was on the *other* side of the law.

"The courthouse?" Karin's mother said with bewilderment as she turned to Cal.

Cal hesitated briefly, then shook his head, laughing. "I was too embarrassed to tell you. I got pulled over for speeding awhile back and I decided to fight it. Got lucky when the cop who issued the ticket didn't show."

Not that you weren't guilty, Karin thought. She was almost disappointed that his brush with the law had been nothing more than a speeding ticket. She had hoped it would be enough to make her mother see him for the loser that he was. Instead, her mother laughed it off as though it was nothing.

As they prepared for dinner, Karin noticed that Cal appeared to have made an effort to look good that evening. His hair was combed, his clothes clean, and he had brought enough pizza to feed four people, even though he hadn't known that Ben would be there. "Call it intuition," he told Karin with a smile. She was surprised to see him help her mother by getting plates and glasses from the cupboard. "I'll set the table," he told them. "You girls just take it easy."

Over dinner, Cal told them stories about his childhood, laughing as he recounted how the snowstorms on the East Coast had been so heavy that his father used to make him get out and walk along the edge of the road so that they could follow in the car without ending up in the ditch. "Never mind that *I* fell into the ditch a few times!" he laughed. "My father figured it would toughen me up. I was small, so I had to work twice as hard to get his respect." He had come from a mining family of five boys and two girls, and he moved away when the mines closed and left the town destitute. He missed his family, he said, but seldom got to see them because of work commitments and the cost of travel. "Maybe you and me could go out someday and visit them together," he suggested to her mother. "Maybe you could come too," he added, smiling at Karin with raised eyebrows. She smiled back, sure that she would never sit in a car with him for the long drive to the coast.

Still, as much as she hated to admit it, Ben may have been right, she decided. Maybe she was judging Cal by his looks instead of trying to get to know him. She felt better just seeing Ben chatting with him, and her mother was obviously even more taken with him now that she had heard a bit about his childhood.

After finishing the pizza, Karin stood and started to clear away the dishes. "Here, I'll get that," Cal said as he took the plates from her hands. "I don't mind doing the dishes." Karin saw her mother make a playful face of exaggerated joy behind his back. Karin couldn't help but smile as she headed to the living room with Ben. Cal *was* making her mother happy. Wasn't that what really mattered?

When everyone got comfortable in the living room later, Karin lifted a DVD from the top of the television, waving it toward the couch.

"Ben and I are going to watch a movie tonight – a romantic comedy."

"Aw, I didn't know you rented a movie," Cal said disappointedly.

"Ben and I have been looking forward to it. We haven't seen all that much of each other lately so ..." She looked at her mother with a pointedly hopeful expression. Perhaps she and Cal would go out for a change.

"There's a fight on TV tonight – kind of an important one." He looked back and forth between Karin and her mother.

"Oh, man, I forgot! It should be a good one too!" Ben answered excitedly. He then saw the expression on Karin's face and stopped talking.

"Mom said you don't like sports," she said flatly to Cal, tapping the movie case against her hand.

"I just like *real* sports. You know, not the stuff your mother watches. Figure skating and everything," he shook his head as though it was hard to believe anyone would enjoy such a thing.

"I'd like to see the movie too, but we can watch it later," her mother suggested as she turned to Karin. "The boys both want to see the boxing."

Ben must have noticed that Karin was getting upset, so he interjected. "I don't mind watching the movie if you want to."

But Cal had already turned on the television and was flipping through the channels. "Look – here it is! Just in time too. Come on, Brenda. Sit here with me." She smiled and reached for her bag of crocheting from beside the chair as Cal threw his hands up. "Not that knitting again! Can't you just sit and watch the fight without doing that?"

Karin's face dropped as she watched her mother put her things down and sit obediently beside him on the couch. "Anything else, Cal? Maybe something to eat or drink?" Karin asked sarcastically.

Ben caught her tone but Cal seemed oblivious to her sarcasm. "That'd be great! Do you have any beer?"

"I'll get it, Karin," her mother said quickly, getting back up. "You sit here with Ben and I'll get us some dessert." She headed past Karin, guiding her toward the chesterfield.

"It'll take more than ice cream to make up for this," she muttered as she took her mother's spot in the living room. Ben reached over and clasped her hand, but it didn't stop her foot from tapping restlessly as coverage of the match began. She pulled her hand from Ben's and crossed her arms, staring at the screen petulantly.

When the fight ended, Cal raised his hand toward Ben in a gesture that clearly read "Gimme a high-five!" Ben smacked his hand and then looked back at Karin with an amused chuckle. Her mother watched them both happily, laughing when Cal jumped up to give her an unexpected hug.

"I won twenty bucks on that match," he announced. *Perfect*, Karin thought. *He gambles, too.*

When the evening was over, Ben got up and said that he should be getting home.

"Can I give you a lift?" Cal asked him.

"Sure, thanks," Ben said. "Saves me a long walk."

"Isn't it *won*derful?" Karin's mother asked her in the kitchen after they had left. "Ben and Cal are really hitting it off. I'm so glad we are all getting along so well!"

"Uh-huh. That's just great," Karin answered, hoping that Ben wasn't really getting to like Cal. That would just be too much to handle. "Mom, this is hard to say, but ... I'm not sure that I like Cal much." She could feel her face start to flush.

Her mother's mouth fell open. "Why not? I

thought you said you liked him."

"I didn't want to hurt your feelings, but I just don't think that Cal is the right one for you. He isn't *the* one, you know?"

"I see. Apparently, you know him better than I do. Well, thank you. I appreciate you caring enough to tell me." Her mother's voice sounded hurt, and Karin knew she had made a mistake by saying anything.

"I'm not trying to interfere, Mom. I just thought you should know ..." Her voice drifted off. "I'm sorry. I guess I shouldn't have said anything."

"I never told you who your boyfriend should be," her mother said pointedly, turning away from her.

"You're right. I'm sorry." Karin crossed the room and hugged her mother from behind. Her mother gave Karin's hand a quick pat.

Even though she wished she hadn't said anything about disliking Cal, Karin couldn't help but think again about his quick explanation for his presence at the courthouse. It didn't sit right with her for some reason. She was sure that she had seen something in his face when Ben had first mentioned seeing him – just a flash of something. Guilt, perhaps? Fear?

As she got ready for bed, the conversation with Cal ran through her mind. *Speeding ticket*, she thought disbelievingly. That old car of his probably couldn't even reach the speed limit. She wondered what he had *really* done.

Chapter 6

Over the next few weeks, Karin had to admit that Cal was proving to be devoted to her mother, driving her wherever she needed to go, helping around the apartment, and working his way into their lives. He even went so far as to call her mother every night as soon as he arrived home from their apartment. That is, when he actually went home. He had started staying overnight sometimes.

After Ben had recognized Cal from the court-house, Karin and Sage had done a web search for anything that might tell them more about Cal.

"We've been doing this forever," Sage had complained. "There are almost 25,000 hits for 'Calvin Etherington' when you Google him, and we've already looked at so many. How will we know which one is *your* Cal?"

"Oh, please don't call him *my* Cal," Karin had answered with a shiver. She took a deep breath and leaned back in her chair in front of Sage's computer. "None of the sites we've checked have anything to do with him. Where else can we look?"

"Try the *Post* or the *Gazette*," her friend suggested. "Maybe they did a story on him, you know, like 'Flasher Strikes Again!' or – "

"You're just so funny, aren't you?" Karin said, but she tried the sites for their local papers anyway. "No. Nothing."

"That's good though," Sage told her, pushing the keyboard away. "It means you're probably worrying for nothing. He may not be the best person for your mother, but he's probably harmless."

"I just don't have a good feeling. Why did he lie about the speeding ticket?" Karin reminded her. She looked at her watch and groaned. "I was going to get so much done tonight and now I'm too tired to even open a book. I'm never going to get my marks up this way."

"I'll drive you home," Sage offered. "That is, if my parents will let me have the car for twenty minutes. I'm practically under house arrest these days."

"At least you don't have Cal in your house."

"You're always looking on the bright side," Sage laughed.

Since then, Karin had resigned herself to the fact that her mother was getting more and more serious about Cal. For her mom's sake, she made an effort to try to get along with him. She just wished that she could stop worrying about him so much. She was having trouble concentrating at school and despite having given up sports, her grades were still falling. She'd have to get her act together soon or her plans for university were going to be impossible to attain. After years of planning for her future, Karin couldn't bear to see it start slipping away.

When the doorbell rang, Karin walked over to the security speaker, heard it was Cal, and buzzed to unlock the lower entrance. Her mother should have been home by now. She could hear his boots on the wooden steps outside as he climbed and turned on the first landing, then the second. She opened the upper door and watched as he came up the last few stairs, pulling off the dirty orange hat that he had worn every day since she met him.

"Hi, kiddo! Boy, the snow out there is getting

really heavy." As if to prove it, he stamped his feet on the top step and chunks of snow from the late-March storm fell loose and dropped down to the landing beneath. Karin made a mental note to tell her mother that Cal should learn to take his boots off at the bottom of the stairs.

"We're supposed to get a lot more. They're saying it'll snow most of the weekend," he continued. She moved her shoes over on the mat so that there would be room for his. Snow was already melting from his treads, leaving dirty wet marks on the tiles under his feet. "Mom isn't home yet. She had to go to Aunt Jean's for a baby shower."

"Oh, I forgot all about that." He hung his coat and headed across to the fridge. "Mind if I have a beer?"

She watched as he took the bottle from the fridge before she could answer. He knew his way around the kitchen as well as she did. "Help yourself," she answered, hoping he would detect the sarcasm.

"You want one?" he asked, as though anything in the fridge was his to offer.

"I don't drink beer."

He chuckled and held one toward her. "You can be honest with me. Your mom might fall for that, but I don't know anyone your age who doesn't suck back a beer like it's water every now and then."

"You do now." Karin felt her jaw tightening.

He put the second beer back into the fridge. "So, who's the baby shower for?" He tossed the beer cap into the garbage and leaned back against the counter.

"My cousin Fiona. She's due in the summer. I had to work this afternoon, so I couldn't go."

"It would have been a drag anyway," he assured her. "Bunch of women sitting around drinking tea and gushing over baby clothes." The room was silent for a moment as Karin chose not to respond. "Kids are a big responsibility," he went on before taking a swig of his drink. "I'm glad I never had any. No offense or anything."

"Some people just aren't meant to have kids, I guess." *And you're one of them*, she thought. *You did us all a favor by keeping your genes in your jeans*. She picked up the electric kettle, making sure there was enough water in it to fill a mug, and plugged it in so that she could make tea. "You were married though, right?" She had asked her mother awhile ago why Cal was still single at forty-one. Karin had been surprised to learn that he had been married before.

"Yeah, I was married, straight out of high school, back east. Dumbest thing I ever did." He shook his head as if he found it hard to believe that he could have been so stupid. "We were both eighteen, just kids. We were hot for each other – figured we knew what we wanted, you know. But her parents really had it in for me. They never liked me, especially her mother who was a real b-i-t-c-h, and they gave us a hard time so we just took off to city hall and got married on our own. We were married for ten years before ..." He stopped and shook his head again and tipped the beer bottle to his lips.

"Wow, married at eighteen. I can't imagine," Karin said, pulling a mug from the cupboard. "That would be like me getting married next year. I don't feel ready at all for that kind of a commitment."

"You've been seeing that guy Ben for a while though, right?"

"Over a year. It's a pretty big deal that I've been with him for so long. I've never found anyone else that I wanted to be with for more than a few months."

"Really? Well, believe me, some guy will be lucky to have you." He sounded sincere, but it still turned her stomach.

"Yeah, right," she said, trying to ease the awkward moment. She laughed and turned to reach into the canister for a tea bag. "I'm no prize. I get really ugly if I have to get up before eight, I'm way too sensitive, and my last boyfriend told me I'm too particular about everything. We'll just see how lucky some guy will be."

She dropped the tea bag into her mug and reached for the kettle. As she started to pour the boiling water, she sensed him moving in her direction. She felt him come up behind her – felt his arms slip around her waist from behind, the front of his body press close, lining the back of hers.

"Anybody would be lucky to have you," he said again. His breath was hot on her neck; her skin froze, her throat closed.

She twisted out of his hold, repulsed, her right hand still holding the kettle of boiling water, her elbow bent. She caught his chest in the center of the ribcage and the impact caused scalding water to slosh from the spout of the kettle.

"Hey, careful!" he warned her sharply as he stepped back, his hands up to shield himself. "You could have burned me!"

"What do you think you're doing?" she demanded, the kettle still in her hand, steam drifting away.

"'Doing?' What do you mean?" he asked, his face the picture of confusion.

"You know what I mean! You touched me!" Her voice rose an octave, quivering.

"Hey, kiddo! Karin! Oh my gosh! I was just giving you a little hug!" His eyes sought hers with pained regret. "I'm sorry, sweetheart, I didn't know you would be so offended." He stepped toward her and then back, hands gesturing, pleading, seeking her understanding. He looked genuinely upset that she would accuse him of anything untoward.

Her eyes narrowed and she held the kettle closer to her chest, using it as a line of defense, feeling vulnerable and afraid. Her heart was pounding and she felt as if her skin had been sanded so that every pore was sensitive, every hair raised.

"It was just a hug," he repeated. "Karin, sweetie, I think of you as a daughter." His dark eyes stabbed at her, still trying to connect with her own. "I thought we were close. You know, close enough that I could give you a little hug and let you know that I'm proud of you."

"You have no reason to take pride in me. You are not my father," she said. "And if you were, I wouldn't want you to hug me like that."

But he had planted a seed of doubt. Was it possible that she was overreacting? As uncomfortable as he had made her feel, she wondered if she had read too much into his action, taken offense at what he may have considered a meaningless sign of affection. She had not been expecting a hug and she was not used to fatherly gestures. It had felt threatening and frightening at the time, but looking at him standing before her now, she saw nothing menacing about him, only a small, insignificant man – a smudge, a loser.

She turned away but stood sideways and poured the water into her mug, conscious of his presence, watching for any sign of a move toward her. He responded by cautiously stepping farther away, backing toward the kitchen table, and pulling out a chair.

They both turned at the slamming of the door downstairs, both listening to the stamping of snow from boots, followed by the slow approach of her mother's footsteps. Forty-two stairs.

"I'm sorry if I upset you," he said quietly again. His calculating eyes were locked on Karin's. He was waiting for her to accept his apology.

She took a deep breath and looked away. *Hurry up*, Mom, she thought, as she willed her up the stairs.

"Hi!" her mother called out happily as she opened the door.

"Hey, babe," Cal answered, making the hair rise again on the back of Karin's neck. He crossed the room and kissed her mother's cheek. "How was the baby shower?"

"Oh, it was so nice! There were lots of people there I haven't seen in awhile. I really should keep in touch with people better." She hung her coat, made her way to Karin, and then reached up to tuck some loose hair behind her daughter's ear. "Everyone was asking for you. They couldn't believe you're already preparing for university."

Karin didn't say anything, prompting her mother to look at her with concern. "Are you okay?"

She looked across her mother's shoulder at Cal. He was looking at her sadly, hands held out, palms up, as though seeking absolution. She watched as he mouthed "Sorry" and shook his head helplessly.

She turned away and scooped the teabag from her mug, tossing it into the garbage can under the sink.

What am I supposed to do now? she thought in confusion, closing her eyes as her mother's naive chatter buzzed unwittingly behind her.

Chapter 7

"I'm serious, Sage. It was so creepy. I keep thinking about it, and I still don't know if I'm imagining that he was pressing up against me on purpose or whether he really was stupid enough to try hugging me that way. Anyway, I've just decided to let it go."

Sage brushed her hair back from her face and then shook her head. She stared across the table in the fast food restaurant where they were having lunch on Monday. "Come *on*, Karin. There is no way he was just *hugging* you. Do you think my dad would come up and hug me that way? That's just sick." She dipped her fries in the ketchup and bit the ends off three at once. "That guy's a pervert. He's probably on porn sites all the time, or has a big stack of gross magazines at his place."

"Thanks for that thought. Now every time I think of him, it'll be a vision of him sitting on the floor in the corner of a dumpy apartment with *Penthouse* centerfolds pinned up on the walls and a slew of magazines spread around him on the floor."

"Ick! Sorry I mentioned it," Sage said as she shuddered. "What did Ben say when you told him?"

Karin looked down and concentrated on folding her paper napkin into an accordion. "I didn't tell him."

"What? Why not?" Sage demanded. "Why would you keep something like that from him?"

"We've been on a little break. I told him I need the extra time to study before we send out our university applications, so I haven't seen him for days." Karin realized she was avoiding the real answer. "He'll be stupid about it, that's why. It wasn't anything. It was a gross hug, that's all." Sage looked doubtful. "It *was*. I'm going to Ben's after work tonight, but I'm not going to tell him what happened. And don't you tell him either. Ben will act like it was a big deal and he'll want to make a huge issue out of it. I just want to let it go. Mom really likes this guy and I guess that's all that really matters right now. She deserves to be happy."

Sage scraped the sauce off the side of her burger before taking a bite. "Your business," she said with her mouth full. "But I think you should give Ben a chance. You should be sharing this with him. And I wouldn't be surprised if Cal does it again. If I were you, I'd tell my mother."

"You're not me," Karin reminded her.

"Good thing. I think you're crazy. Just so you know."

"I've always known," Karin sighed. "Just save me some fries, would you, Monkey?"

When the girls got back to school, Sage headed for gym class and Karin walked to English with Isabelle. They had been fairly good friends when they were on the basketball team together, but now, as Isabelle chatted away about their last game, Karin found herself distracted, remembering how she had dealt with the Cal situation. When her mother had asked if she was okay, she could have said no and explained what had happened. Her mother would have been upset, might have demanded that Cal leave, but she might also have lost any self-confidence that she had gained over the past six weeks that she had been dating Cal. Instead, Karin had answered that she was "fine" and she had almost heard his sigh of relief from across the room. She had saved his sorry ass. She hoped it wouldn't come back to kick her in her own one day.

As she and Isabelle entered their classroom, Karin realized that she hadn't heard a word of what her friend had said. Somehow, nothing Isabelle had to say seemed important anymore.

* * *

Arriving at Ben's house after work that day, Karin carefully avoided any mention of Cal. She had no way of knowing that his mother would raise the subject.

"Ben tells us that your mother is seeing someone," his mom said brightly. Ben was digging around in the cupboard for a snack for Karin, who was sitting at the table flipping through a magazine.

"Yes. She's been seeing him for a while." She avoided looking at Ben's mother. She really didn't want to talk about her mom's relationship.

"We should have all of you for dinner sometime," his mom suggested. "I've been wanting to meet your mother. I'm sure we'd have a lovely time together."

Karin's heart stopped as she tried to envision

Cal and the Garcias spending an evening together. "Maybe," she answered. She would have to find an excuse if a date was ever suggested.

"You'll meet them at graduation," Ben said casually, and Karin looked at him gratefully. Graduation was still two months away. Anything could happen between now and then, she thought.

When Ben's mother had left the room, he put a bowl of pretzels on the table and sat down, leaning toward Karin urgently. "I learned something today," he told her, glancing toward the door to be sure his mother was gone.

"What?"

"Remember how Cal told us that he had been at the courthouse because of a speeding ticket?"

"Yeah?" She leaned closer, urging him on.

"I was talking to Dayton Pierce this afternoon. He got a speeding ticket a couple of months ago and he was telling me he went to court to fight it. The thing is, he said traffic tickets are dealt with at the annex building beside City Hall."

Her mind raced. "What do you mean? Where did you see Cal?"

He took her hand. "At the other courthouse, the big one up at the top of the hill. They don't handle parking fines or speeding tickets or jaywalking violations. They deal only with the major stuff."

"Major?" she demanded.

He nodded. "They only handle criminal offenses. It's the criminal court."

Her face blanched. "I have to tell my mother! She's going to be devastated."

"But that's a good thing, right? You've been wanting her to break it off with him."

She nodded. "I just hate to see her get hurt." She picked up a pretzel and bit into it distractedly. She hoped she could find a way to tell her mother that Cal had lied about his reason for being in court, without causing her too much heartache.

* * *

The next morning, Karin carried her toast and juice into the living room to have breakfast in front of the TV. She shuffled across the carpet in her slippers, her oversized T-shirt hanging down to her knees.

"You look exhausted," her mother observed from the couch, putting her crocheting down as Karin joined her. She pulled the blanket from the back of the couch and spread it across so that it covered both of their laps. "Aren't you sleeping well?"

"Not really," Karin said. "I need to talk to you about something." Her voice caught nervously. There was simply no good way to break the news.

"Schoolwork stressing you out?"

"No, that's not it. But university apps do go out soon." She could see that her mother was edgy about something as well.

"I need to talk to you about that. About you going away in the fall."

"Oh, Mom, if you're worried that I won't get the scholarship ..."

Her mother shook her head. "No, it's not that. It's just, well, the point is that you *are* going away soon and that I could be here on my own."

"I know. I've been thinking about that too. I mean, I want to make sure that you're going to be all right," Karin started, relieved that her mother had given her an opening to talk about Cal.

"I can't imagine this apartment without you – it would feel so hollow. Empty nest syndrome, I suppose – that's why I need to talk to you. To let you know that Cal is going to move in with me. With us."

Karin's face reflected the horror she was feeling. "Move in?"

"It just makes sense financially that all of us

live together," her mother continued, picking nervously at an uneven fingernail.

"*All of us*? What do you mean, *all of us*? You mean, he's moving in before I leave in September?"

"You know that neither Cal nor I earn all that much, and we're paying rent on two places, plus our heating costs, our telephone – "

"But do you love him?" Karin asked with concern. She realized that there was no acceptable answer to the question. If her mother *didn't* love him, how could she let him move in with them? It would be pathetic and wrong. And if she *did* love him, well, *how could she*?

Her mother hesitated before answering cautiously. "That's what I hope to find out. I like being with him. And it isn't like we're getting married – not right now. We're just moving in together."

"But should you do that? When you aren't even sure if you love him? It doesn't sound like something you'd recommend to Ben and me."

"Look, I know you don't like Cal much – " Her mother sounded slightly irritated.

"It isn't just a matter of not liking him." Karin decided she had better divulge all of her concerns now, before it was too late. "This is hard to say, but he gives me the creeps. He *looks* at me funny, and he hugged me once."

"Oh, Karin, for goodness' sake."

"I mean he *hugged* me, way too close, and besides that, I think he may have a criminal record. He was at the courthouse – "

"At the courthouse? You mean when Ben saw him? He already told us that was a speeding ticket!"

"But it wasn't. It was the criminal court, not the traffic fine division."

"Criminal court?" Karin's mother frowned. "What are you talking about?"

She told her mother all she could, but she knew that everything she was saying was speculation and instinct.

Eventually, her mother raised her hand in frustration. "All right, Karin. Cal will be over this afternoon and I'll talk to him about it. In fact, I'll let *you* talk to him about it. Let's get it out in the open. But I want you to promise me that when we're finished talking and we're satisfied that he isn't some kind of monster, that you'll stop trying to ruin this relationship for me. I'm really disappointed that you are trying to make him look so bad. Just because you don't like him – "

Karin opened her mouth to protest but then

said nothing. She took a deep breath. "I just want to know that this is right for you."

"Of course it's right for me," her mother answered, sounding relieved. She leaned over and hugged Karin. "I'm *excited* about him moving in. I wanted you to be excited for me too. He's a good man, and he loves me."

Karin nodded, but she was already looking ahead to Cal's visit in the afternoon. They would have their little chat, and maybe, finally, they'd find out what Cal Etherington had been hiding before he could weasel his way into living with them.

Chapter 8

Cal sat with his head in his hands, his elbows resting on his knees. "I was hoping I'd never have to get into this," he told them. "It isn't something I'm proud of."

Karin looked across triumphantly at her mother and watched as her face sagged in anticipation of what he might have to say. Feeling guilty for having taken pleasure in knowing she was right, Karin rose from her chair and went to sit on the arm of the couch, putting a hand on her mother's shoulder.

Cal sank back on the opposite end of the couch and sighed. "It was a mistake. I've made a lot of them, and I'm not going to lie about it." He looked as if he was considering how to tell them about his past. "I used to drink," he admitted. "A lot. In fact, if you had known me a few years ago, you'd have known a different man than I am today. I wasn't working, I couldn't seem to get a break, and I didn't have a lot of hope that my life was ever going to look any better than it did right then. So I started drinking. It wasn't so bad at first, but soon it got to be all that mattered to me. I can't tell you much about that time of my life because frankly, I can't remember many details about it."

He half-laughed and looked across at Karin and her mom for support. Karin stared back at him coldly, but her mother was hanging on to his words, leaning toward him with a frown.

"There was a real dive where I used to hang out – just a cheap bar over on Reynolds Street – and I got to know all the other regulars there. We were pretty close – most of us were going through some hard times. We had no family, no money. We helped each other out sometimes, bought each other a drink when we could. Anyway, this one guy, Donny, came in one night and was already pretty drunk. He came up to me and he started in about how I owed him some money for something or other, and I didn't know what the hell he was talking about, you know what I mean? I tried to ignore him, but he wouldn't let it go and he just kept getting in my face. So finally I gave him a shove, just to get him away from me. And Wes, the owner, told us to take it outside. To tell you the truth, I don't even remember *going* outside, but then there we were and he's punching my face and I can feel that he's cut me under my left eye – that's how I got this scar," and he pointed at the faded crescent-shaped scar beneath his eye. "So I started hitting him back and soon we were both down on the ground and there were a bunch of people watching us, and then the cops came and the next thing I know, we're both hauled off in cuffs."

"This was a few years ago?" Karin's mother asked worriedly.

"Almost a year and a half. The courts are busy, so it didn't get heard until February. Anyway, that whole fight was a wake-up call for me. I've never been a fighter. Look at me! I wouldn't win in a fight against a kid, never mind a man bigger than me! But the booze made me tough, made me lose my perspective, you know?"

Karin watched in amazement as her mother nodded.

"I got help, Brenda. I knew that I couldn't do it alone, so I turned to Alcoholics Anonymous. One day at a time, and all that stuff. Went to AA meetings for months. Folks there helped me to see that I was on a path to destruction. So I gave it up."

"Gave it up? You drink beer here," Karin pointed out.

"One or two, now and again," he agreed. "But I've got it under control, see? No more heavy drinking for me. I'll never let myself get so low again. And I came out of court with just a year's probation. First time offense. I proved to the court that I had been for help, changed my life, found a job, cleaned up. I'm a new man. I am *not* the guy who used to hang out at that bar. I know what's important now, and it isn't the booze." He sat forward and took Karin's mother's hands into his own. "It's you. You're what really matters." His face pleaded with her for understanding, and Karin watched in disbelief as her mother's reserve crumpled before her.

"Oh, Cal. I wish you had told me all this before."

"I couldn't, Bren. I was embarrassed – ashamed. I wanted you to know me the way I am now, not the way I used to be." He looked down and squeezed her hands. When he looked up again, Karin could see tears in his eyes. "That part of my life is over. I'm just sorry that you both had to find out about this. I didn't want either of you to think any less of me."

"Less of you?" Karin's mother sniffed. "After you've turned your life around this way? No. I couldn't be more proud of you." She reached forward and the two of them hugged tightly, then sat back against the couch together. Cal touched her hair tenderly.

"I should be thanking you, Karin. It's good that you asked about all this." Cal wiped an eye quickly and then his nose. "I don't know what you might have been thinking of me if we hadn't had this talk."

She nodded knowingly and rose from the arm of the chesterfield. "You're right," she agreed, as she met his eyes deliberately. "I have a *much* better picture of you now."

"Karin!" her mother chided.

She ignored the obvious embarrassment she was causing her mother and waved a hand dismissively toward them both as she left the room and walked over to the coatrack.

"Don't run off," her mother pleaded in a low voice, coming after her into the kitchen as she pulled her jacket on.

She turned to her mother impatiently and responded in a loud whisper. "Isabelle has talked about her uncle before. He's an alcoholic and he hasn't had a drink in over four years, but he still goes to AA regularly."

"It doesn't mean that everyone with a drinking problem has to attend meetings forever," her mother sighed.

"Isabelle said her uncle's afraid that if he has one drink, then it may lead to another, and then ... Doesn't it bother you that Cal drinks beer when he's here? I don't think it's right." Her voice had risen to a level that Cal was sure to hear.

"He has it under control, Karin. I have *never* seen him drink too much."

"I just don't think – "

"For God's sake, Karin! Let it go! You've done everything possible to ruin this relationship for me and I'm tired of it. Cal is trying his best to get along with you and you just keep on finding fault with him. It's extremely selfish of you. You'll be leaving for school in a few months anyway."

"You don't get it, do you?" Karen hissed, leaning toward her mother. "My grades are falling. Everything I've worked for is starting to look like it could just disintegrate because I can't concentrate – *because I can't stand Cal*! If I don't get that scholarship, I may *have* to stay home, here, with you *and* with him. Wouldn't that be great? Me, you, and Cal. One big, happy family!" Karin's shoulders dropped in defeat, her eyes filled and she looked away and shook her head helplessly.

"I'm sure you're just blowing this all out of proportion," her mother said, reaching for her arm. Karin shook her off as though it hurt to be touched. Her mother stepped back, biting her lip. Then her face hardened with resolve. "Cal is going to move in here next weekend, with or without your approval," she said stiffly. "And I want you to help him with the move. It's the least you can do to welcome him here."

"But I don't want him here," she reminded her mother sadly as she zipped her jacket, then turned and trotted down the stairs to get away from them both. *It's them against me now*, she thought bleakly as she walked down the street with nowhere to go. She and her mother had been so close once.

After several hours of wandering alone, she finally came home to find Cal's car was gone. Her mother must have asked him not to spend the night. And Cal was conspicuously scarce over the remaining days before he was to move in. It was as though they were granting her this short hiatus.

* * *

The following weekend, at her mother's urging, she helped them both carry loosely packed boxes of Cal's few possessions up all the stairs.

"Is this really all you have?" Karin asked as she lifted a box from the back of the truck.

He opened his arms grandly toward the truck. "Years of my life, all shoved into a dozen boxes and a couple of garbage bags. Doesn't say much for me, does it?"

She shrugged. "I just expected more, that's all."

"He left most of his furniture in the room he was renting," her mother explained to her as she joined them at the back of the truck. "We didn't have room here, and someone else may want it."

"I doubt that," he laughed. "It wasn't worth anything. I got most of it at the second-hand place downtown."

Karin followed Cal up the stairs with an open box of old VHS movies, some envelopes, magazines, and a pile of loose photographs. It was hard to imagine that someone his age could have so little to show for his life.

"Who's this?" Karin asked him as she

dropped the box onto the kitchen table and noticed the photograph of a young woman sticking up from inside one of the books. She pulled it out and noticed that the girl was not much older than herself, with brown eyes, dark skin, wavy hair, and a wide grin.

Cal took the picture from her and ran a finger over it thoughtfully. "My wife," he said. "First year we were married. Looks like you, a little." She studied the picture in his hand and had to admit he was right. He dropped the picture back into the box and carried it to the bedroom. Karin rested her hips against the kitchen table and wondered what Cal had been like in those days and what his wife had found to smile about when she looked at him.

"Do you think we should find ourselves a bigger apartment now that we have two incomes paying for one place?" she heard her mother asking Cal from the bedroom.

"Are you kidding? This place is way bigger than my old place, and once Karin leaves for school in the fall, it'll be plenty big for the two of us. Why waste our money on space we don't need?"

Karin was relieved to hear his response. If anything ever happened to her mother's relationship with Cal, she was sure that he would leave and her mother would end up having to absorb the additional rent on her own. A pessimistic attitude, she chided herself, but it was hard to look at anything related to Cal as being very positive. She went back down the stairs and checked to see what else needed to be carried up from the truck. Glancing into the cab, she was startled to take note of an empty beer bottle on the floor.

The reality of the situation was impossible to ignore. Karin's head ached as she walked slowly back up the stairs empty-handed. The man was an alcoholic, a possible criminal, and a liar, and her mother was blind to it all. As much as she wanted to protect her, nothing Karin said was going to make a difference. All she could hope for now was to get that scholarship somehow and get as far away from home as possible. She couldn't bear to think about the alternative.

Chapter 9

Over the next two weeks, Karin learned what life with Cal would be like. When he had stepped out of her mother's room one morning after he moved in, Karin had taken note of his bleary eyes, his unbuttoned shirt, and his rumpled hair. She had raised her chin defiantly, stared him in the eye, nodded once, and went into the bathroom. Closing the door behind herself, she turned the lock with a deliberate and satisfying motion, holding the doorknob with firmly clenched fingers until she heard his steps retreat down the hallway.

Sometimes it felt as if his eyes were following her and she would turn to see him in the doorway or in his usual chair in front of the television. There was nothing to confirm that he had been staring at her – no reason to accuse him of anything at all.

Once she had been taking a bath and after tying her robe tightly, had opened the door to find him standing there, so close that she almost walked straight into him.

"Holy mother of ... what are you *doing*?" she demanded, pulling the collar of her robe tighter to her neck. "You scared the crap out of me!"

He chortled and moved back a step. "*You* scared *me!*" he snorted. "I didn't know you were in there."

The tub water ran noisily down the drain, glugging every few seconds. "Yeah, I can see how it would be hard to hear that," Karin said. "Excuse me."

She walked by him and into her room, closing the door and ensuring that she could hear it click tightly behind her. There were no locks on the bedroom doors. She wondered if she should speak to her mother about that. She stood with her back against the door and surveyed her bedroom ruefully. It was a mess. Even Pippy's cage was overdue for a cleaning. *Nothing* seemed right anymore.

"He's at it again," she said without unnecessary greetings when Sage picked up the phone shortly thereafter.

"What, the lurking? The stalking?" Sage had heard every detail of his every move since he had moved in the month before.

"Yeah. It's like he's a cat and I'm the mouse. I know he's after me, but I don't know when I'll come around a corner and find him ready to pounce."

"Is your mom blind? You know you can come and stay here anytime you want."

"I've told her over and over, but he doesn't do it when she's in the room with him. Now she thinks I'm just saying things to make her kick him out. The more I complain about him and ask her to make him leave, the more she's convinced that I'm paranoid. And it isn't just that. I don't like the way he talks to her lately."

"What do you mean?"

"She came home late from an appointment last week and he grilled her as though she'd been cheating on him. She ended up crying, so then he apologized, brought her a coffee, and rubbed her feet. He's like Jekyll and Hyde. I don't know how she stands it. I can't stand it."

"Why isn't she listening to you?"

Karin got teary. "I don't know. I was complaining about him last night and Mom actually said that it was a good thing I'd be leaving for college soon."

"She's probably right. It's already May and you'll be out of there at the end of August. It's only a few months."

Karin was quiet for a moment. "A few months. I hope I can keep escaping him that long." She looked across at Pippy, who was running as fast as he could go on his exercise wheel, expending tons of energy but getting absolutely nowhere.

* * *

"On your way to work again?" Brenda asked on Friday evening as Karin shut off the bathroom light and walked into the hallway. Karin had barely been able to find her lip gloss in the bathroom. Since Cal had moved in, the cabinet and the drawers seemed to overflow with shaving cream, disposable razors, uncapped toothpaste, and disgusting toenail clippers.

"Yeah. Jeff had to take the night off, so I picked up his shift." She walked down the hall and got her jacket. Her mother stood leaning in the doorway and pointed to the window where a driving rain was hitting the glass.

"Maybe you should let Cal drive you," Brenda suggested. "It's pouring out there and you'll get soaked."

"I've always walked in bad weather before. I'll be fine. Where's that massive umbrella we used to have?"

"That's crazy talk," Calvin said firmly as he came out of the living room. "There's no reason to walk when I have the car right there." He took his coat off the hook, and slipped his arms into the sleeves as though the matter was closed.

"I said I'm fine." Karin's voice was sharp.

Brenda twisted the ring on her right hand nervously. "Cal *wants* to drive you, Karin. Please let him do this for you."

Karin huffed in undisguised exasperation and started zipping her coat angrily. Halfway up, the zipper caught on the nylon, bunched on one side, jammed stubbornly, and became more and more impossible to move as she yanked up and down in frustration. Calvin watched with amusement until her mother stepped forward to help. Karin raised her hand to stop her then looked across at Cal with a tight jaw.

"Fine. Let's go then." She walked out the door without a goodbye and started down the stairs. A moment later she heard his steps behind her. *It's only five blocks*, she said to herself. *Five blocks. It won't kill me.* She sped ahead of him down the stairs, grateful for the gap she was creating between herself and Cal, whose feet were taking each step with controlled deliberation. She clutched her jacket closed and stepped out into the teeming rain, trotting quickly to the passenger side of the old car and climbing in, glad that the door wasn't locked. She kicked aside an empty coffee cup on the dirty floor mat.

Cal jumped in the car, slammed the door, and flipped the safety lock. Rubbing his hands together, he shivered and watched the rain beating on the windshield. "It's getting worse. You call me later when you're ready to come home and I'll pick you up. No need to be walking home in this."

Karin didn't reply. He put the key into the ignition and turned on the defroster. "It'll just take a minute to get the steam off the windows." She knew that he was looking at her. She concentrated on wiping water from her purse. "You know, you should think about getting your driver's license now that my car is here for you to drive. I don't mind lending it to you. I'll even give you lessons and save you from going through Driver's Ed. No use wasting your money on that." He turned on the wipers, and she looked up to watch them sweep across the windshield. "I don't know anyone your age who doesn't drive."

"I don't drink, I don't drive – jeez, I'm just not normal, right, Cal?" She wondered how long it would take for the windows to clear so that they could go.

He laughed and reached across to pat her shoulder. She instinctively shifted her body away from him and could sense his irritation as he hesitated and then dropped his hand back to the steering wheel. There was a moment of awkward silence before he put the car into reverse and backed onto the road.

Even though it wasn't yet five o'clock, downtown traffic was starting to flow away from the main street. Heavy clouds gave a false impression of a much later hour; the sky was black. Headlights glared on huge puddles lining the uneven surfaces of the poorly maintained streets. Winter's garbage blocked the storm drains. Cal pulled up to the stop sign at the corner of their street and then waited as a slow line of cars followed an overly cautious driver. The wiper blades slapped back and forth rhythmically, steadily, breaking the silence between them in the car. The left blade was torn, and the rubber hanging loosely from the metal wiper left a wide smear across the driver's side of the windshield.

When the way was clear, he swung the car sharply onto the road. The fast turn was unexpected and Karin felt her body shift left and her weight fall toward him.

"Whoa," he said laughing, and reached across to support her by placing his hand on her arm. She leaned upright quickly and felt his hand leave the outside of her sleeve. Then it repositioned itself on her thigh.

"Get your fucking hand off of me!" she demanded. His hand did not pull back.

"Oh come on, Karin. I'm not going to hurt you." His hand did move slightly then, the palm turning a fraction of an inch, the fingers twitching, then sliding upwards, pressing gently but deliberately.

"Stop it! Let me out of the car." She flung his hand away from her and grabbed the door handle. Her voice became shrill. "Pull over! Now!"

"All *right*, all right! No need to make a big deal of it! You want me to get into an accident or something?" He checked the rearview mirror and slowly steered over to the curb.

She pulled on the handle once, twice, pushing her body against the door. "It's locked – it's locked!" she shouted, before her head cleared and she pushed the lock-release button and then tried the handle again. This time the door swung open and she leapt out onto the street. Hanging on to the open door, she leaned down and looked across the car at him. In the muted illumination of the car's yellow ceiling light, he looked jaundiced and small.

"Bastard!" she spat at him, then slammed the door and stepped up onto the curb. Pulling her coat tightly around her chest, she strode resolutely down the sidewalk toward work.

Chapter 10

"I'll kill him!" Ben yelled into the phone.

"No you won't," she sighed, surprised by how calm she felt. She was relieved that Ben hadn't doubted her when she called from work and told him what had happened. "I need to deal with this myself. And I have to convince my mom that it happened. She hasn't been listening to me. She's oblivious to what he's really like. She's just so thankful to have someone paying attention to her. She agrees with everything he says. How could she have fallen for such a creep?"

"You should call the police and report him for sexual assault," Ben told her firmly.

Karin took a deep breath. "I thought about that. It's just that ... it wasn't really *assault*, was it? It was a hand on my leg, not a violent attack. He didn't grab my breast or anything."

"It's still assault."

Karin sat back on the stool behind the sales counter. One of the lights above her may have had a loose connection; it flickered erratically and made it difficult to focus, causing her to feel slightly dizzy. "You're probably right. But I have to talk to my mother first. I can't have the police suddenly show up at her door without her even knowing what has happened. How would she feel?"

"How would *she* feel?" Ben repeated with astonishment. "Does it really matter?"

The door of the convenience store swung open and a young couple came in, shaking water from their jackets. "I have to go," Karin said reluctantly, her mouth close to the receiver. "I'll talk to you later."

Ben seemed hesitant to let her hang up. "Do you want me to come down there?"

"I'm fine, Ben. There isn't anything you could do. Thanks though."

"Why don't you come here after work tonight? I'll come and get you. You can stay in the spare room."

"No, I'd better go home and talk to my mom. I'll be fine. But thanks. I really do have to go."

"I love you."

"You too," she answered softly, watching as the young couple approached the front of the store. "Bye."

The customers placed their purchases on the countertop and she smiled and ran their newspaper and the loaf of bread through the scanner and chatted mindlessly with them about the rain. The bell over the door rang hollowly as they left the store. It was a quiet night, too wet for most people to be out, and she turned her head toward the door quickly the few times that it opened, praying that Cal wouldn't come and try to talk to her.

At eleven, Mr. Lee came in to help her balance the cash register and clean up the store for the next day. "Do you have a ride home?" he asked as he shut the cash drawer and locked the till before turning off all but the night-lights.

"No, I'm going to walk. But thanks." She pulled on her coat and headed out the door, holding it open behind her as he followed her out.

"You sure? It's still pretty wet out here."

"I'm sure. Sometimes I think it's safest to walk." He looked at her quizzically. Karin knew that he must be wondering why she would hesitate to accept a ride on a night like this. He had never given her reason to be afraid of him.

She barely noticed the rain on the way home. Her mind was too preoccupied with thoughts of how to tell her mother about the car ride. It would be devastating for her, but Karin was past caring. Maybe this was the blow she had needed to make her come to her senses.

When she arrived home, the apartment was quiet. Her mother and Cal were in bed, the apartment dark except for a light over the kitchen sink, which was always left on for her when she was the last home at night.

As much as she wanted to talk to her mother right then, she decided not to chance waking her in case Cal woke as well. The talk needed to be with her mother alone. If Cal was there, he'd confuse her mother with lies.

Sleep was impossible as she envisioned scenario after scenario of her mother's possible reactions to the news that Cal had assaulted her.

She turned on the bedroom light and picked up her chemistry notes. If she wasn't going to sleep, she might as well try to study.

At 3:45 in the morning, she realized that concentration was impossible. She closed her book. Her mind simply couldn't absorb one more thing. She picked up the phone and dialed Ben's number, praying that his cell phone was in his room and that his parents wouldn't hear it ringing at this hour. When she reached his voice-mail, she hung up without leaving a message and tried again.

"Hello?" he answered groggily on the second ring.

"Could you talk me to sleep, please?" she asked. "Just talk about anything – anything at all." She shut off the light, burrowed into her blankets, and pressed the phone between her pillow and her ear.

As Ben spoke quietly about his day, she finally gave in to exhaustion and fell asleep.

* * *

Karin and her mother sat at opposite ends of the faded couch in the living room the next morning. Cal had gone to the scrap yard to see if he could find a new muffler for his car. Karin wondered if he had deliberately gone out to avoid facing her. Whatever the reason, she was thankful to have time alone with her mother.

The words were barely out of her mouth when her mother stopped her.

"I already know all about it, Karin. He told me." Her mother's face was tired and expressionless.

"You know? He *told* you he put his hand on my leg?" She fell back against the couch and stared at her mother doubtfully.

"Of course he told me. He was very concerned that you'd been upset with him."

"Damn right I was upset. He was squeezing my thigh!"

Her mother leaned forward and placed her hand gently over her daughter's. "It was a mistake, Karin. I can see how you might have been confused. He told me he tried to keep you from falling over when he turned the wheel too quickly – it's a natural response for a driver to try to shield their passenger from getting hurt – so he reached over and his hand fell onto your leg. He told me that he was embarrassed when it happened. Quite embarrassed."

"So he *squeezed* my leg *by mistake*? Ran his fingers *up my leg* by mistake? Is that what you think? Do you think I don't know the difference between a slip of the hand and a deliberate feel?" She grabbed the pillow from the couch and squeezed it mercilessly into her chest. "I'm not a child, Mom. My instincts are good, and my judgment has never been wrong. Cal is lying to you."

Her mother looked away and studied the

African violet on the side table. The early sunlight was shining on the only plant that they owned, and a couple of small purple flowers hung limply on damp stems that were weakened from over-watering. She pulled a yellowing leaf from the bottom of the plant and toyed with it, tearing unconsciously at the edges.

"Why do you keep him around? Because you feel sorry for him?"

"I told you. He's good to me. You've seen how he treats me. Like I'm a princess." Her mother tore the yellowed leaf in half and dropped the pieces onto the edge of the saucer that sat under the plant. "He told me once that I'm every-thing his first wife wasn't."

"Oh really?" Karin said dryly. "Like blind to his faults? Like willing to believe everything he tells you?"

She glared silently as her mother drew her feet up onto the couch to hug her knees. She noticed her mother's mouth twisted slightly before she answered.

"I love you, honey, but I believe Cal when he says that what happened last night was an accident."

"So you think I'm lying?"

"No, of course you're not. You're telling me

what you *think* happened. But it's just your perception. That doesn't make it true."

"So you're taking Cal's side again," Karin stated flatly.

"Oh, Karin. It isn't a matter of taking sides." She avoided her daughter's eyes. "He's worked very hard to make a new life for himself. He deserves a chance."

"He's had his chance. You have to ask him to leave."

Her mother gazed down at her hands. "Don't make an issue of this, honey."

"*I'm* not the one making an issue. Cal has made the issue!" Her heart pounded as she leaned toward her mother and tried to control her anger. "I'm telling you, I can't live here with him. Are you going to ask him to go or do I have to move out?"

When she was met with silence, she straightened and turned to walk toward the hall. Stopping in the doorway, she turned back and added, "I really should apologize for what I've thought of him in the past. I had thought he was a sleazy, pathetic, stupid little man. But he isn't pathetic or stupid at all. He's really quite clever, isn't he? Clever enough to tell you all his sordid lies and make you believe them. You're so desperate that you're willing to accept anything he says as the truth. One really has to wonder, just who *is* the most pathetic?"

She spun away from her mother's pained expression and hurried down the hall. Pushing open the door to her bedroom, she headed straight to the closet and bent down to dig past the shoes and the boxes of old schoolbooks for the duffel bag that she used to carry to basketball practice. She opened the top drawer of her dresser and grabbed several pairs of socks and underwear, a bra, and her pajamas. She shoved that drawer closed and pulled out the next, snatching a fitted top and a sweatshirt. Then she crossed the hall to the bathroom and pulled her makeup bag from the bottom drawer.

"What are you doing?" Her mother's voice sounded exhausted. She was standing in the doorway, watching her daughter take the shampoo from the side of the tub.

"I'm going to Sage's. She knows all about what Cal has been doing, and she told me I could come stay with her anytime I needed to. Ben knows too. And he knows what happened last night – he wanted me to call the police, but I didn't want to do that. I wanted to talk to you, and give you a chance to stand up to him. For me.

I guess I was kidding myself." She zipped her bag and pushed past her mother. "Feed Pippy for me. I'll come pick him up when I can get someone to drive me."

"Karin, don't go – please."

Karin looked back at the worn face, the gray eyes that were filling with tears. "Will you ask him to leave?" she asked her mother.

"I can't."

"You can, Mom. You just won't."

In the ensuing silence, she leaned forward and brushed her cheek against her mother's, then turned and headed out the door. No footsteps followed her own down the hallway. Her mother didn't try to stop her.

Karin barely noticed the houses or the people that she passed, barely heard the traffic. She had never been so angry or so hurt.

Her mother had let her walk out the door, and now she'd be left living alone with Cal, without the ability to see him for what he was. There was a chance that her mother could be in danger, and Karin was no longer there to help her.

She tightened her grip on the straps of her gym bag and quickened her stride. *She's made her choice*, Karin decided. Sage was right. It's her mother's problem now.

Chapter 11

"Your marks are definitely suffering," Mr. Pettipas told Karin with concern a few days later as he leaned toward her from behind his huge desk. "I know you've been having some problems, and that you aren't living at home now."

"How do you know that?" Karin asked stiffly.

He leaned back in his chair. "Your mother called me and said you were staying with the Lewises. She was worried about you – concerned that you may be under some stress."

She laughed hollowly. "Did she tell you why?"

Mr. Pettipas looked surprised. "I assume because of your entrance requirements for univer-

sity. I know that you've been struggling lately."
He opened a file folder on his desk and ran his
finger down the top page. "And your marks cer-
tainly aren't at a scholarship level at this point.
You've always had very high expectations of
yourself and I know it was your intention to get
into one of the better schools." He coughed
uncomfortably when he saw her eyes starting to
fill. "I'm not telling you that I want you to pull up
your marks," he assured her. "I'm just worried
about you, Karin, as is your mother. Something
must be bothering you. When a smart girl like you
starts getting Cs ..."

"I'm fine," she said. "Just having a little trouble concentrating. I'll try to do better." She stood
and took her books from the corner of his desk,
swaying slightly as a wave of nausea and dizzi-
ness came over her.

Mr. Pettipas looked at her with growing concern. "Are you all right?"

"I'm fine. Can I go now?"

"Of course. But if you need to talk ..."

She nodded and turned away, her face
flushed. He was right. Her marks weren't good
enough. She'd have to study harder.

That evening, after sorting through her
mixed feelings, she picked up the phone at Sage's

and dialed her mother's number.

"Karin?" Her mother asked without saying hello.

"Hi, Mom. Mr. Pettipas said you were worried about me. I just wanted to let you know I'm fine." She was sitting on the day bed that Sage had in her room for the occasional sleepover. Although she had slept there many times in the past, it felt strange to be there on a more long-term basis now, and hearing her mother's voice made her realize she missed her. "I wanted to give you the number here in case you need me. In case anything happens."

"I'm fine, Karin. I've got the number already. Are you sure they don't mind you being there? I mean, I don't want to be imposing on Sage's family this way – "

"You're worried about imposing?" Karin shook her head and felt her eyes fill. "They don't mind. They want what's best for me." She was sure the inference would not go unnoticed by her mother. "I was there yesterday while you were at work and I picked up Pippy and most of my clothes. The Lewises have invited me to stay here until I leave for school in September. If you want to meet for lunch sometime or go anywhere, just you and me, then let me know."

She heard her mother's voice soften. "Of course, I'd love to see you, honey. That would be good. Though I really wish you would give Cal – "

"I love you, Mom." She hung up the phone and stared at herself in the smudged mirror over Sage's dressing table. The puffiness around her eyes made them look hollow.

* * *

She had been living at Sage's for over two weeks and had been studying constantly, barely coming up for air.

"I wish I could see you more," Ben sighed, his arm resting across the back of her seat at the movie theater. He had practically forced Karin to go out with him for the evening, showing up at Sage's, taking the schoolbooks out of Karin's hands and leading her to the door as she groaned about having no time for a movie. Sage had come trotting after them, after begging her parents to let her out of the house. For once they agreed.

Karin sat between the others as they waited for the show to start, the three of them chewing red licorice that they smuggled into the theater.

"I never have any free time," Karin moaned to Ben. "Sage's house is more than half an hour away from work by bus so I'm losing a ton of time every day. Her parents are really nice and if it works out right, then they pick me up or drop me off. But usually they're just too busy for that. Besides, they do enough for me already and I hate to ask for rides. Between that and our exams coming up soon – "

"Don't remind me!" Sage groaned. "Although, ever since I was grounded, my marks have gone way up. Now I just want to see how well I can do. Since Karin moved in, my father has even let Sulley come over to study with us a couple of times."

"You must be happy about that. The last I heard, your dad wanted you to be a nun," Ben said.

"You know what?" Sage asked excitedly. "My parents are starting to accept Sulley! He's been trying to talk to my dad more and they've found out they have some things in common. I sat and did homework last week while the two of them watched TV together. I think they might actually *like* each other!"

Karin turned to her impatiently. "Of course they do. What's not to like? They're both great people."

Sage's face twisted into a grimace. "Hello?

You *have* met my father, the keeper of the virgin? Earth to Karin, earth to Karin. Have you forgotten how strict and controlling my father is?"

"You *made* him that way, Sage," she answered irritably. "Give him a break! He really loves you and let's face it, you're a high-risk daughter. You're willing to try anything, and I mean *anything*, for a thrill. You drive too fast, you sneak out your window at night – "

"You make me sound awful. I'm just trying to have some fun." Sage pouted, then started to giggle. "And I *do* have fun when I can get away with it." She reached for her wallet. "I'm going to get popcorn. Anybody want to share a big greasy bucket with me?"

"Not me," Karin said.

"No surprise there," said Sage. "You never eat anything anymore. Mom thinks you don't like the food at our house."

"I'll share with you," Ben told her, and Sage clambered over another couple toward the aisle. He turned back to Karin. "My mother noticed you've lost weight too. She thinks you look too thin."

"She should stop playing doctor all the time," Karin snapped.

"She *is* a doctor and she's worried about

you," he answered gently. "She thinks you need to start taking better care of yourself. I really wish you'd go and see someone. Your face is pale, and Sage tells me that you're not sleeping well. You're always jumpy and your mind wanders."

Karin tipped her head back and closed her eyes. "Sorry. I just wish everyone would leave me alone."

"You don't need to apologize," he said patiently. "You've been through hell. I just want you to get better." They sat in silence until Sage came back and the movie started.

A few minutes later, in the intimacy of the darkened theater, Ben reached across as he often used to and placed his hand on Karin's leg. She instinctively tensed, pulling away as she caught her breath. His hand leapt back from her as though it had been scalded and he leaned toward her ear to whisper. "Oh my God, I'm so sorry, Karin. I shouldn't have done that. I just wasn't thinking."

"It's okay," she assured him numbly.

"No, really, I – "

"I said it's okay." She took his hand and squeezed it reassuringly, avoiding his face. She could feel his eyes on her as she stared at the screen and tried to concentrate on the movie. She thought that if she could get caught up in the action on the screen, maybe she would forget everything else for just a while. But later, as Ben and Sage talked animatedly about what Karin assumed must have been a good movie, she could barely recall who was in it.

After Ben dropped them off, the girls said goodnight to the Lewises and headed to their room.

"Still time to do homework for an hour or so," Sage's father called after them jokingly as they headed up the stairs.

"Still time for you to finish cleaning the garage," Sage jabbed back teasingly.

When the girls were in bed and the lights went out, Karin spoke quietly in the comfort of the darkness. "You don't know how lucky you are to have parents like yours." Her voice trembled slightly and she took a deep breath before continuing. "I've never actually told you how awful my father was."

"What do you mean?" Sage asked, rolling over and looking across the room in the dark.

"He never really cared about me. I always had to be on my best behavior when he was home because Mom was so worried about everything being just right for him. I had to be quiet and polite and clean all the time – invisible really – while he spent most of his time criticizing my mom, telling her what to do and when to do it. If she didn't do something the way he liked, he'd yell at her, get right up in her face, sort of like he was threatening her, and make her do it again. I used to run and hide in my room."

"Oh, Karin. How awful!"

"I had a blanket and pillow in my closet and a whole pile of stuffed animals. I'd just curl up and pretend that I was somewhere far away. I figured if I stayed out of his way, then he wouldn't be so angry with Mom. The day he finally left home was almost a relief for me. But Mom didn't take it that way. She just fell apart. I hated him for it."

Sage turned on the light over her bed and looked across the room at her friend. "Shit, Karin. Why didn't you ever tell me that before?"

She curled up and tightened her hold on the pillow. "Because he's gone. It's over."

"You mean you don't carry that around with you all the time?" Sage sounded doubtful. "I heard crap like that can affect you your whole life."

"Not me," Karin said firmly.

"That's good." Sage still didn't sound convinced. "But what about your mom?"

"I don't know," Karin admitted. "I wanted to think that she had come a long way, you know, raising me on her own and getting a new job. But now, with Cal ..." She pulled her pillow closer and her voice became muffled. "I just don't know what's happened to her."

"It's like she doesn't think she can do better," Sage said quietly.

They both lay in silence.

"Are you going to be okay?" Sage asked finally.

"I don't really want to talk about it anymore," Karin answered.

"Oh. Okay. But if you ever want to talk – well, you know you can. I'll always be here to listen."

"I know. Thanks, Monkey."

Sage turned out the light and rolled over. Within minutes, Karin could hear Sage's breathing become steadier and deeper. Her own chances of getting any sleep were slim – how was she supposed to sleep when her mind was filled with all of these memories as well as the fear that her mother could be reliving all of these things again and who knows what else?

The next morning, Sage's mother was reading the Sunday paper when the phone rang. She answered and then passed the phone to Karin, mouthing "Your mother?" questioningly.

"Karin?" her mother said with nervous excitement. "I want you to come home. I've asked Cal to leave!"

"What? Really?" Karin was astonished.

"It's true. He left this morning. And he won't be coming back. I miss you, Karin. I should never have let you go the way I did. You're the most important person in my life."

"And Cal is really gone?" Karin asked cautiously.

"Yes."

Karin thought she heard a hesitation, as though there was more to be said, but her mother continued. Karin pushed aside any questions and made the decision quickly. "Okay. I'll be home in a couple of hours." She put the phone down on the table and looked at Sage and her mother with a "Who would have guessed?" shrug. Her lips twitched with a smile of relief.

"He's gone?" Sage asked bluntly.

"That's what she tells me." She looked at them both with a growing giddiness. She couldn't stop herself from smiling. She practically danced her way up the stairs to Sage's room.

"We're going home, Pippy!" she said, poking a finger through the cage and petting the hamster's soft fur. He responded by checking her finger tips for food.

As she finished packing her clothes and gathering her other possessions into a borrowed laundry basket, she began to question the wisdom of her decision to go home. The hurt that her mother had inflicted was not going to be easily forgotten. Her mother had believed Cal over her, and allowed her to leave home rather than lose him. Was it even possible to rebuild a relationship with her mother after that, or would this entire experience leave a wedge between them that could never be removed?

And why had her mother and Cal suddenly ended their relationship? She felt her skin start to prickle. What if he wasn't actually gone? Her mother had been blind to the truth about him for so long that it seemed almost too good to be true that she should suddenly have come to her senses.

Karin closed her eyes and took a deep breath. "I'm getting paranoid, Pippy," she said. "Come on. Let's see if Sage is ready to drive us home."

Chapter 12

Karin walked home from school on Monday, comfortable to be back in her own neighborhood, even with its peeling paint and weedy lawns. She had never felt entirely relaxed when she was at Sage's, although she would miss the late night chats.

She was surprised to find the door unlocked downstairs when she got home. "Mom?" she called as she climbed the steps to the kitchen.

"Hi. I'm just making coffee. Do you want some?" Her mother was standing at the counter dressed in track pants and a sweatshirt.

"No, thanks. Why aren't you at work?" Karin asked. "Did you get off early?" The phone rang and she stopped talking and turned to answer.

"Don't!" her mother warned loudly. Karin drew her hand back in surprise. "It's Cal," her mother said.

The two of them stared at the phone as it rang a third time and was picked up by voicemail. Within seconds, they could see that the message light didn't blink. Whoever it was hung up.

"How do you know it's Cal?" Karin asked worriedly.

"He was fired today and he blames me – even though it was probably because he wasn't getting the sales he needed. He'd had warnings about that before. He came out of the manager's office and walked straight over to my desk. Told me that I had set him up to be fired, that I had complained about sexual harassment. I hadn't, and I told him that, but he blamed me anyway. They had to come over and tell him to leave. He was escorted out."

"Someone at work must have complained about him or he wouldn't have suggested that," Karin thought aloud.

"I don't know. I just know he is angry with me. He called me a few times at the office after he left. I finally just couldn't take it anymore and stopped picking up. I told the manager about it and she told me to go home. Now he's calling here."

"How many times has he called?" Karin asked, staring at the phone as it started to ring again.

"I don't know. I've been home for an hour and it's rung maybe seven or eight times. I answered the first time, and he left a few messages after that. I've saved them. Now he just hangs up."

Karin picked up the phone and listened to the messages. Cal's voice sent a chill down her spine.

"Are you happy now? First you kick me out of the house, then you get me fired. No one screws with me that way. No one."

"Oh my God, Mom ..."

The call ended and Karin stared at the floor as the second message began. "Brenda? Are you there? It's me again. Look, I'm sorry. I just ... I love you and I want you back and ... I mean, I got nothing left, right? I stayed in a shelter last night – you don't know how awful that is. I need you. I need to talk to you. That damn company! They tell me to get out, and they don't care, they don't give a damn about what *I* say, or what *my* side of the story is ..." his voice rises, the words come faster. "I know you lied to them. I know you said something to get back at me for ..." There was some muttering, then a clatter as though the phone was dropped. The message ended.

The next message was controlled and business-like. "Hi, Brenda. I left a few things at the house. Can I come by and pick them up sometime? Let me know."

Karin hit the *talk* button to create a busy signal for inbound calls, then stuck the phone in the kitchen drawer. "Nice talking to you, Cal," she said.

Her mother smiled, but her face still looked worried. "I think he's been drinking. If he doesn't stop bothering me, I'll have to get a restraining order."

Karin saw that she was serious. "Don't just think about it. Do it."

"Give him twenty-four hours to sober up and get past it," her mother said wearily. "I expect he'll settle down."

"You really have to stop making excuses for him. Especially now," Karin told her impatiently. Her mother's eyes filled with tears. "But at least you finally got up the nerve to tell him to leave. That's the main thing, right?" Her mother nodded and wiped her face. "Come on. I'll make us some tea," Karin offered.

Later, as she turned out the lights in the living room before bed that night, Karin thought she caught sight of someone standing under the streetlight across the road. She instinctively moved out of view, flattening herself against the wall. Her heart pounded as she peered around the corner of the drapes. The yellow streetlight shone through a thick mist. No one was there.

She shook her head and left the window. *My imagination is running away with me*, she thought. *Maybe Ben is right. Maybe I do need to get some help.*

* * *

She was up early the next morning, cramming for her English exam. When it finished at eleven, she walked home in the sunshine, grateful for the half day off and the afternoon to herself. The warmth of the spring day made everything seem more positive. But as she rounded the corner onto her street, she slowed and felt her throat close. Cal's car was in their driveway, its wheels halfway up the lawn, the driver's door open. She hesitated, then started to walk quickly, trotting across the street. Her mother was at work, so she knew that Cal must be in their house alone.

The landlord came around the corner of the

house with his hedge clippers and frowned at Karin as he saw her approaching. He waved toward the car with disgust. "Look how he left his car!" he said. "Tell him to move it before I have it towed."

"Sorry, Joe. He shouldn't even be here," she explained, opening the door to her apartment without having to use her key.

She ran up the double flight of steps, pulled on the inside door, and ran up the carpeted stairs to the kitchen. "Hey! Get out of our house!"

She couldn't see him but could smell the alcohol. Anger overshadowed any better judgment she may have had to just leave. "Cal? Where are you?" she called, marching into the living room, then down the hall to her mother's room. She swung into the doorway and glared at him where he sat on the floor in front of the dresser, the drawers open, contents in disarray.

"What do you think you're doing?" she demanded.

"Hey, Karin," he said without looking up, continuing to look through the bottom drawer. "Shouldn't you be at school?"

"What are you doing here? Mom told you she didn't want to see you again."

He raised his eyes and met hers, narrowing

them as he took in her furious expression. "I left some things here," he said, turning back to the drawer. Your mother kicked me out before I could get my stuff together." His words were slurred, his hands clumsy as they indicated the pictures and papers that were scattered across the floor. "I thought I'd better come when no one was here. She doesn't want to see me."

"How did you get in?" she demanded.

He reached into his pocket and held up the spare key. She snatched it from his hand and wondered how her mother could have been so stupid as to not insist on getting it back.

"Just hurry up. Get your stuff and go," she said, pulling a half-empty box toward her as she squatted to gather the papers from the floor. She reached out and picked up some photographs – Cal and his family, she assumed as she glanced at a group of children in dated clothes, their sullen faces focused on the photographer. She slid a few photos into a pile and dropped them in the box. Cal with his brothers, Cal with his wife. She looked at the picture with confusion, taking in the familiar face, the one so like her own, and the unfamiliar body that was unmistakably pregnant.

"What's this?" Karin asked, sitting back on her heels and holding the print out accusingly. "I thought you said you never had any children."

He took the picture from her, looked at it for a moment, and then crumpled it in his hand, tossing it back onto the floor. "I didn't. It died."

Karin couldn't help but feel a twinge of pity for him and she wondered if his drinking was related to the loss of the baby. "I'm sorry," she said, and when he didn't respond, she went back to sorting the mess on the floor. She glanced down at some papers of her mother's – bank statements, phone bills, electricity notices – and placed them aside to keep.

A thick brown envelope was lying open by the foot of the bedpost. She reached over and picked it up, then looked across at Cal. He was busy reaching under the bed for some rumpled clothes. She hesitated and pulled the package of legal papers out, flipping through the pages quickly.

"What are you doing?" Cal snatched the papers from her hands and looked down to see what she had been reading. His jaw tightened. "You just can't keep your nose out of anyone's business, can you?"

"I was just helping you to get your things together," she retorted, pulling herself onto her feet with the help of the bedpost. She indicated the box to him and he tossed the envelope into it angrily.

"It's your damn interfering that made your mother kick me out," he said accusingly, jabbing a finger at her. "After you left, all of a sudden she started judging me. Telling me I was drinking too much. Then the first time I slipped up with her, she started saying that 'Karin was right, Karin had told me all along.'"

"What do you mean, *slipped up with her*?" she asked.

His eyes narrowed as he recounted the incident. "She didn't tell you? She probably realized it was nothing anyway. All I did was give her a little shove. I hardly touched her, but she fell down and made a big deal out of it."

"You hit Mom?" Her hand tightened on the bedpost as she suddenly realized how dangerous it had been to confront him here. Cal had been drinking, they were in the apartment alone, and he couldn't be trusted. She stepped back from the bed and edged toward the door. "Just get your stuff and leave. We don't want any more trouble."

He snorted cruelly. "Trouble? You think I haven't had anything but trouble because of you already?" He got to his feet, kicking the drawer so that it half-closed, askew on one side. "Me and your mother would have been fine if you had just kept your mouth shut." His eyes were slits, his body tensed. She realized with growing nervousness that he was losing control.

"Get out of our house," she heard herself demanding as she backed slowly toward the door. She put her hand on the doorframe and edged evenly out of the room. "Get out or I'll call the police!"

"You little ..." he stammered, before lunging toward her as she started racing down the hall, pushing away from the corner, to the head of the stairs.

She ran and was barely at the stairs before he caught her wrist, gripping it so tightly that she knew she could never get free. He grabbed her other wrist and twisted them both until she shrieked, then he pushed her up against the wall and crushed her arms against her chest. "It was *your* fault," he spat at her. "Told her I had *touched* you, like you hadn't been asking for it all along. Even though she said that she believed me, I could see her looking at me differently. It wasn't the same. She started to judge me, started to give me a hard time. I was just trying to be nice to her, trying to *love* her."

"I – I didn't lie," Karin choked. "And I didn't

call the police. I could have, but I didn't."

"They fired me from that half-assed job. All women. All those supervisors were women. Said I'd been making people uncomfortable, looking at them funny. Like *looking* at someone is against the law," he spat.

Karin's hands were throbbing. She turned her head away from his face.

"You're a lying bitch, just like all women, just like my ex-wife. Sneaking around, packing her stuff and trying to run off in the night. She deserved what she got."

"Let me *go*!" Karin ordered through gritted teeth as she raised her knee quickly to his groin. He shouted in pain and released her wrists. She flew down the stairs and opened the door to the landing, but her foot caught on the loose carpeting and she fell through the doorway and to the floor in a heap. The ceiling spun above her.

And then his feet were pounding down the stairs after her, and she felt him push her against the floor. She knew he was above her – she smelled his alcohol-soaked breath. Her throat was tight and she heard a muffled cry from a distance and realized hopelessly that she had made the sound herself.

Chapter 13

*K*arin's head ached.

"Don't move, honey. You've got a nasty concussion." Her mother's face was full of sympathy.

Karin winced, as much from the memory of what had happened as from the pain.

"You stay with her," Ben's mother said soothingly from beside the stretcher. "I'm just going to talk to the doctor who attended to her. Ben, you come out to the waiting area for a while. Give Karin a chance to be alone with her mom." She left the room and walked down the hospital corridor briskly.

Ben kissed Karin lightly and left her side reluctantly. Her mother waited, watching as a ward nurse and an orderly moved Karin carefully from a stretcher to a bed.

"I'm just going to get you another blanket and a cup with some ice chips," the nurse told her gently. "Do you need anything else?"

Karin wanted to answer, but they had given her something for the pain and it made her head feel as if it was filled with rubber. Somehow, talking seemed too great an effort.

Her mother pulled a chair up beside her bed and took Karin's hand into her own. "I'm so sorry, honey. You must be hurting so much," she whispered.

Karin tried to nod, but she wasn't sure her head actually made any motion. "Uh huh," she answered, her voice sounding as if it was coming from somewhere else, from across the room perhaps. She suddenly flinched as Cal's face crossed beneath her closed lids. She licked her lips slowly and forced herself to speak. "Did ... they get him?" she asked from the ceiling. "Did ..."

And her mother may have answered, but it didn't matter. The effects of whatever drugs the doctor had given her were working, and she slept.

* * *

When Karin got home from the hospital the next day, the full extent of the situation became clear.

"The police tell me he had served time years ago for domestic violence," her mother told her heavily as they sat at opposite ends of the couch, Karin's feet on her mother's knees. "His wife had tried to leave him. She was pregnant at the time and she ended up losing the baby. He served five years."

"Oh my God!" Karin's stomach turned as she pictured the pretty woman in the photograph. "They should have put him away forever."

They sat silently, both knowing that the risks they had taken were far greater than they had perceived. "He could have really hurt one of us," Karin finally said flatly.

"That's all I've been able to think about," her mother said as she started to cry. "It's my fault. I brought him into our home, I believed in him, I trusted him." She sniffed and reached for the box of tissues on the coffee table and wiped her eyes angrily. "I'm so sorry. It makes me sick to think what would have happened if Joe hadn't run to check on you. He heard you scream."

Karin's dark eyes winced and her mother's chest tightened.

"I'm just lucky he did." Karin's voice trembled. "Who knows what Cal was going to do? He looked so ..." She closed her eyes and tried to block his face from her mind. "If I had just called the police when Ben first told me to."

"Don't blame yourself for this," her mother pleaded as she wiped tears from her face. "I'm the one who let you down. I should have listened to you, I should never have kept seeing him when you felt so strongly about him. I should have known that you were right about him."

Karin turned onto her side and clutched the blanket up to her chest. It *was* her mother's fault, she thought bitterly. She had spent her life putting up with an abusive husband and then had thought so little of herself that she had found another equally destructive relationship. *She put me at risk*, Karin thought angrily, her head starting to ache again. *And I was so anxious to have everything work out for her that I didn't act enough on what I knew. I'm as screwed up as she is.*

Karin's tone was listless. "I think it's time for us to get some help. Both of us. We need to work through why it all happened. If we had just dealt with everything that Dad left behind instead of pretending we were fine ..."

Her mother huffed, snatched another tissue from the box and blew her nose. Her chin jutted out. "Well, I can promise you one thing. I won't be having another man in this house. We were happy here, just the two of us. I don't know what I was thinking to even consider seeing someone."

Karin's laugh was empty. "Happy? Were you really happy?" Her mother pulled the pillow from the couch and toyed with the tassels, *just the way she did when Cal was here the first time*, Karin thought. She sat up and reached over to squeeze her mother's hands. "Look. You made some lousy choices. Dad, Calvin. But not *all* men are like them. Look at Ben – he's been right there for me all along – and his father is so great. And Sage's dad too. But you ended up with Dad and with Cal, and avoiding men for the rest of your life isn't going to resolve whatever problems caused that, or the ones that resulted from it."

"I don't want to see a psychiatrist," her mother said, looking hurt.

"I didn't say it had to be a psychiatrist, but I think we both need some kind of counseling. Do you realize what we did? We both fell right back into the pattern we were in with Dad. You settled for someone who paid attention to you, even if that attention was controlling and belittling, and if you had stayed with him longer, I bet he would have ended up as abusive to you as he was to his first wife. And I'm just as guilty, because I could see it, I could sense it, but I tried not to make waves, not to get too involved. I ran to my room, ran to Ben's, and to Sage's. I hid from what was happening. I should have *made* you see."

"I don't know."

Karin dropped her mother's hands. "You don't *want* to know. Look at us. I should have called the police right after he assaulted me in the car. And you should have called when he left those horrible messages. We knew we should have, but we didn't. Why? Why didn't we call?"

Her mother bit her lip and turned away.

"Exactly!" Karin said with disgust. "You can't give me an answer. Don't you think it's important that we know *why* we ended up in this mess? Or do you want to do the same thing again and again? Is that the way you want me to see you? As a victim?"

She saw her mother's face flinch as though she had been struck, but she couldn't stop. "What does it take, Mom? Do you want me to end up just like you?"

"No!" her mother blurted, tears streaming down her face. "All I ever wanted was for you to be something more, something *better* than me. I just didn't know how. I didn't know."

They sat silently for a moment, divided by an experience that should have brought them together.

When Karin spoke, each word was deliberate and firm.

"You know now."

Chapter 14

The view of the courthouse at the top of the hill was partially blocked by the autumn-colored leaves on the trees in the park below. It had been months since Cal had been arrested, but both Karin and her mother had thought about him all too often as they waited for this day to arrive.

Ben took Karin's hand and squeezed it as they walked up the path. Sage followed a few steps behind with Karin's mother.

"You look good," Sage said as she took in the way Karin's clothes fit over her healthier-looking shape.

"I hope you're talking to me," Ben teased, and Karin surprised herself by laughing.

"Thanks," she told Sage. "And thanks for coming with us."

"I'm sure it'll all be very *Law & Order*," Sage predicted.

Karin's mother, dressed in a new black skirt and sweater, walked silently, lost in thought. When they were nearly to the top of the hill, Karin took her mother's arm and let Sage and Ben walk ahead of them to the steps.

"Are you ready?" she asked her mother, before taking a deep breath.

"Ready or not ..." her mother quipped with an uneasy smile, and they stepped up and went through the door that Ben held open for them. They climbed the staircase inside and when they reached the courtroom, they stopped for a moment, took a deep breath and looked at each other. Reaching across, Karin's mother tucked some loose hair behind her daughter's ear.

"There's Joe," Ben pointed out as he ushered them into the room. Their landlord was dressed in a navy suit, and was pulling at his tie uncomfortably. They walked down the short aisle and slid into the row behind him. Karin placed her hand on Joe's shoulder and when he turned to smile at her affectionately, she leaned forward and kissed his cheek. "How're you doing?" she asked him warmly.

"I'll be better when this is all over," Joe

admitted.

"We all will," she agreed and sat back next to her mother.

In time, a door opened at the side of the courtroom and Cal was escorted in. He looked even smaller than he had the first time Karin had seen him. His suit was too big for him, the hems hanging in folds over his shoes, the collar several inches too loose around his thin neck, the sleeves wide over his clenched hands. If he had been sallow before, now he could only be described as sickly. His skin was as folded and as loose as his clothes. He swaggered as he was escorted across the room toward his lawyer.

Despite his unthreatening appearance now, Karin felt her stomach knotting and a sweat start to prickle the skin beneath her arms. *He's nothing*, she reminded herself. *He's nothing*. But as he approached the table where he would be sitting, he looked up and scanned the faces in the courtroom, and his eyes met her own for just an instant before they slid deliberately across her shoulder to rest with obvious insolence on her mother's face. Karin heard a sharp intake of breath next to her as Cal's lips twitched and parted, sneering dismissively. Then, in an instant, he turned his back to them, as his lawyer leaned across and whispered something. The moment was over.

"That s.o.b.!" Karin whispered to Ben, who responded by rubbing her knee. "I hope he really gets what's coming to him." Sage's hand squeezed her shoulder and she felt her mother's hand take her own. The four of them sat there together, silent in anticipation of seeing justice done, and for the first time since Cal came into their lives, she felt that she and her mother were strong.

On his lawyer's advice, Cal pleaded guilty to reduced charges, but because of his previous record, he received the maximum allowable sentence. It was all they had hoped for.

After leaving the courthouse, Joe invited everyone out to dinner. He told them again that he would never forget what it had felt like to come around the corner and see Karin on the landing with Cal over her. He had pinned Cal against the stairs and held him as he waited for the 911 operator to alert the police and an ambulance. He had made sure that Karin was moved safely into the vehicle before calling her mother at work.

"I'm getting too old to go through anything like that again," he told them at the table.

"You're my hero, Joe. Like Superman, or

Batman," Karin told him.

"Do I have to wear tights?" he asked, looking down at his heavy mid-section with dismay. "Maybe I should skip dessert."

* * *

The next day, Karin and Sage met for lunch before heading back to university.

"So what's your residence like?" Sage asked as she bit into her taco.

"*So* small," Karen moaned. "I hardly have room for Pippy's cage, and we're not even supposed to have pets there – but I wasn't going anywhere without him. Anyway, I'm not complaining because I'm just lucky to have been accepted by the school at all. You know, if Mr. Pettipas hadn't recommended me so highly for this scholarship, I may not have made it."

"He never did *me* any favors," Sage reminded her.

"You didn't do a whole lot for him either," Karin laughed. "I think you took more of his time than the rest of the whole senior class." She took a sip of iced tea and looked thoughtful. "I can't believe how much more focused I am this year than last."

"What would you have done if you hadn't been accepted?"

"You know what? I'd have been disappointed, but now that I have a better idea of what's important in life, I think I could have waited and just tried again next year. I'm realizing that success isn't always measured by marks or how much you can earn. It's who you are, how you face life, and how you grow from your experiences."

"Oh, gag me! And I'm the one who's going to be studying psychology!" Sage laughed.

"I learned that in counseling," Karin admitted.

"No kidding. What about Ben? Is he happy in his new place?"

"Yeah. I really miss him though. It's going to be *years* before we're done with school."

"Well, he's only an hour away," Sage reminded her. "And you still see him on weekends."

"We try, but he made the tennis team, and I'm back playing basketball – "

"That's great! I thought you were going to go crazy without your sports." Sage's voice dropped off.

"Me too!" Karin said, "I should never have given up what I loved doing most. I needed that distraction, or even just that whole endorphin release, to keep me going. Anyway, our weekends are pretty busy, but Ben and I try to get together even if it's just for a few hours, and we're still in touch every day. He texts me all the time, and we talk every night before bed. You know, I had never given him credit for being so understanding. He really came through for me."

"Do you think it'll work out with the different schools and all the hot guys you're meeting?"

Karin threw a straw across the table. "Very funny! No, this whole experience made us even closer. I told him things that I'd been keeping to myself and it's made him understand me better. Ben and I are in this for the long haul. What about you and Sulley?"

"Same school, different classes. I thought I'd see him every day, but I don't."

"But it's still good between you, right?"

"Yeah, for now. Dad actually seemed kind of happy that the two of us ended up at the same university. I think he'd rather I was away from home with Sulley than away from home and single. Too many unknown guys."

"I'm surprised you aren't bringing one or two home just to drive your father insane," Karin teased.

"Not yet." Sage was quiet for a moment. "Seriously though, how *is* the counseling going?"

"Okay, I guess. It's hard. I have another appointment next week."

"What about your mom?"

"I worry about her. I really wish that I could help more, but it's difficult when I'm not there. I did convince her to go for counseling at the Women's Health Center. She's only been a few times so far, but they have her in a group with other women who can relate to what she's been through." She sighed as she remembered what her mother had told her. "She has a lot of issues. Some of them go right back to her childhood and her own relationship with her parents. She isn't going to get better overnight, but then, nothing worth having comes easily, right?"

"Another quote from your counseling sessions?" Sage groaned.

"Worse. It's from your best friend Mr. Pettipas!" Karin admitted, and they both laughed. "I'm *so* glad those days are behind us."

"Ditto," Sage agreed. "We're moving on – to bigger and better things." She held her bottle of iced tea up.

"To better things," Karin echoed with a huge smile, before tapping her bottle against Sage's.

Need more **NJPP**?
Check out:

The "Not Just Proms & Parties" Series

Drama, comedy, love, revenge ...
like life, only juicier!

Here's a sneak peek at
Belinda's Obsession

When I was dressing to meet Candice, I thought that I would arrive early at the café, that I would seek out a table facing the door, and make sure that a candle was lit so that it would soften my features and make me look less "before" photo. I would order myself a hot chocolate so that I had something to hold, so that I wouldn't just be sitting there like a desperate single girl who is doing nothing but waiting. I thought that I would be sure to sit straight and tall so that my figure would be passable and so that I would appear confident. I would watch for her to come and I would try not to jump up and run to her like a puppy that had been alone in the house all day. I would smile but keep cool, not grin like an idiot until my face ached. No matter how much the mohair of my sweater made my neck itch, I would not scratch.

But Candice is here already, sitting in the chair I would have chosen at the candle-lit table I'd have wanted, and she is watching the door as I come in, smiling the smile I wish I could smile.

I hang up my coat, run my hands through my gelled hair, fall into the chair across from her and put my face in my hands.

"Oh my gosh, what's wrong?" Candice asks

me with concern.

"I just saw my mother," I sigh, and my voice sounds like a huge, hopeless groan, pathetic enough to make a passing waiter look over at me and stop next to our table.

"I'm sorry," the waiter says, obviously taking my sigh as a complaint about the service. "Can I get you something?"

"Something for a headache would be good," I joke, but he looks as though he isn't sure if he should laugh. "Maybe just a hot chocolate," I say, and he looks relieved.

"Your mother," Candice says. "Is there something wrong with seeing your mother? Didn't she know you were coming here?"

"No, no. It isn't that." I look around to see if anyone is nearby and then lean on the table, moving my face closer to hers, which should be exhilarating but is lost in the mess of emotion that is hanging over me like a cloud from a nuclear explosion. "It's not about me. It's about my mother. She was with a *man*." My voice is low, but I hear it catch on my words.

"So?" Candice looks confused.

"Not my father."

Belinda's Obsession
ISBN-13: 978-1-897073-62-9

Also available from the **NJPP** series:

Chelsea's Ride
ISBN-13: 978-1-897073-44-5

Will Chelsea's self-centered ways ever catch up with her?

"... a truly selfish and conceited character which makes for an enjoyable read as you wait for her to get just desserts ..."
– Lithe Librarian, blogspot.com

"... one of those books that every teenage girl can relate to."
– Teen Adviser, Danbury Library

"Seriously great titles you should check out ..." – *Toronto Star*

Rica's Summer
ISBN-13: 978-1-897073-45-2

Rica learns that revenge can come at a steep price.

"... girls will identify with Rica's low self-esteem, constant comparisons with others ... the fast-paced plot will appeal to readers." – *Resource Links*

"There are many reasons to recommend the 'Not Just Proms & Parties' series ... realistic and interesting ... A quick read with a positive message." – yabookscentral